# THE WIND UNDER
# THE DOOR

# THE WIND UNDER THE DOOR

Thomas Calder

*For Tatiana and my parents*

# CHAPTER 1

The driveway required a sharp turn. A man in a tuxedo with skull face paint waved them forward. Ford rolled down his window.

"Gate's another quarter mile up," the skeleton told Ford. "It'll be open."

"Grace Burnett invited us," Ford said.

The man nodded absently. "I'm just here directing cars."

"You said a quarter of a mile?" Ford asked, embarrassed.

"Unless they moved it," the skeleton said.

Ford took the incline. It leveled off once they reached the gate. Lenny pressed his forehead against the passenger side window, leaving a streak of white clown makeup on the glass. Rhododendron and bamboo narrowed the driveway. Ford flashed his high beams just as the home came into view. The stone property stood three stories. Fifty or so jack-o'-lanterns lined its porch rail.

Ford hadn't seen Grace since their drive up the parkway. They'd briefly kissed at Craven Gap, but a yellow Mitsubishi Mirage loaded with teenagers blasting Adele's "Rolling in the Deep" interrupted things. He and Grace laughed off the awkward exchange. They'd only known each other a month, having met by chance on Ford's fortieth birthday. Grace was not yet thirty. (Somehow *not yet thirty* sounded a lot better in Ford's mind than *twenty-nine*.)

"Now see this here's that Texas money," Lenny said, gawking at the house.

"This isn't her place," Ford reminded him. "It's her uncle's."

"Who's her uncle again?"

"I have no idea," Ford said.

Another tuxedoed skeleton waved them down with a neon green glow stick. The man repeated himself three times before Ford realized he was valet.

At the front door Lenny paused, scrutinizing Ford. "I'd go with Hook," he said.

The comment confused Ford.

"Hook's more interesting than Jack Sparrow," Lenny continued. "Got that obsession with time and that crocodile always after him."

Ford examined his costume. He had purchased the pirate outfit earlier that day. The getup, outside of the hair extensions and hat, could have passed as a slightly exaggerated version of his everyday attire.

"I don't have a hook," he told Lenny.

"That don't matter," Lenny assured him. "If you say it like you do who's gonna question it?"

Lenny's logic annoyed Ford.

"If it doesn't matter, why don't *you* tell people *you're* Hook?"

"But I'm a clown, brother," Lenny said. "I wear it every year."

"So I've heard," Ford said, impatient with the conversation. Lenny had mentioned his costume's annual appearance several times on the car ride out.

Adjusting his large bow tie, Lenny said, "Ain't it funny? We're always just repeating ourselves."

Inside, a caterer offered them champagne. Lenny took two glasses. Pockets of people gathered in the living room. A violinist tuned her instrument near the French door that led out to the back porch. The furniture had either been removed or the room had always gone without. A fog machine cut everyone off at the ankles.

Lenny handed Ford a glass. Bubbles rose to the surface.

"I've been good lately," Lenny said, nodding aggressively. "And I want to keep it that way. But I ain't fooling nobody saying I come up Pinchot Creek Mountain to watch other folks have fun. You with me?"

"I need to find Grace."

Lenny took hold of Ford's left shoulder, turning him about-face. Ford expected to find her standing there. Instead, Lenny pointed toward the kitchen. A bartender served a concoction from a large cast iron pot.

"No one's stopping you," Ford told him.

"You gonna have me go at it alone?"

"What alone?" Ford asked, gesturing toward the crowd.

Lenny considered Ford's point and then headed for the kitchen.

A man in green surgeon scrubs with bloodstained gloves approached Ford. He wanted to know if Ford had seen Al. Ford told him he didn't know who Al was. The surgeon waved him off dismissively.

Another guy in a mechanic coverall with a carjack through his skull called out, "Captain Jack Sparrow! Killer fucking party!"

Ford raised his champagne flute in a lackluster toast. But the mechanic had already moved on. Placing the drink on an end table, Ford scanned the living room for Grace. There was no point, he quickly realized; he had no idea what she was dressed as.

The rest of the band arrived, joining the violinist. The four huddled together and assessed the room. The upright bass player flagged down the caterer, who had switched out her champagne flutes for Jell-O shots. The group toasted before scooping the treats out with their fingers. Afterward, the trumpet player introduced the band. They opened with "Bringing Mary Home."

As people from the back porch hurried inside, Ford edged his way to a corner.

"Captain Jack!" a man dressed as the Joker shouted on his way to the bar. "Why so serious?"

The upright bass player climbed the side of his instrument to the audience's delight. Ford ran his finger over a nearby globe. The weight of its balance was broken, leaving it permanently upside down.

"Sparrow, you seen Al?" shouted a man wearing only a diaper and bib.

"Who the hell is Al?"

The man-baby rolled his eyes.

The band broke into a bluegrass version of "I Put a Spell on You." People from the back porch continued to pour inside.

The temperature had dropped noticeably. Ford's breath billowed out into the tense night air. The muffled sounds from the living room carried through the French door. He was alone.

Grace had only been in Asheville since August. Ford couldn't imagine how she already knew so many people. Could he and Lenny be at the wrong house? He pulled out his phone to text her. But there was no service.

"You sick of your own party?"

Ford spun around. A tall, older man in a cowboy hat stepped out from behind the shadows with a cigar in hand. He paused as he approached Ford. "My apologies," the man said, holding up his hands. "Thought you were my nephew. Same costume."

"I know you," Ford said, returning his phone to his back pocket.

The man's face held the same dull, self-assured expression that stared down from a pair of billboards in town. But it was his imperial mustache and bushy yellow eyebrows that gave him away.

"Al's Pawnshop," Ford said.

The man nodded dully. "I thought of dressing up as something different, but I figured this is as good as any."

The two shook hands. Al held Ford in his grip. His eyes narrowed with suspicion. "You friends with one of my employees?" he asked, studying Ford's face.

"Grace Burnett invited me."

Al's grip tightened. "How do you know my niece?"

"I've got a studio in the River Arts District," he said, matching Al's force. "I've been working on a piece for Grace."

Al released Ford. "She having you paint her or something?"

"I don't do portraits," Ford answered.

Al squeezed Ford's shoulder, pressing his thumb into Ford's clavicle. "She'd be pretty to paint, though, now wouldn't she?"

"Albert!" a woman's voice called from a side patio partially blocked by a large gas grill.

Al drew on his cigar, letting out a deliberate line of smoke in Ford's direction. "Got us a private party going if you're interested."

Around the corner a small fire blazed. The woman wore a blonde wig, an oversized coat, and a silver glittered tutu. In her hand she held the neck of a broken champagne bottle. Her body convulsed with laughter. She was much younger than Al. Younger than Ford too.

Al introduced her as Bethany from Houston. "And this young man is Captain Jack Sparrow, in so far as I can't remember his name."

Ford introduced himself. Bethany continued to laugh.

"I'm s-s-sorry," she said. "It's just—Al, I broke it. I broke the bottle. I've been sipping from a broken bottleneck this entire time."

"Miss Bethany here's a wild child," Al said with a broad grin. "And a bad influence."

Bethany held out a joint. "You want?" she asked Ford.

Ford declined. "You flew in from Houston?" he asked.

Bethany nodded.

"Sit down," Al commanded Ford. "Makes me nervous, a man standing like that."

The chair's cold metal pressed through Ford's costume.

Bethany passed the joint to Al. He took a hit. Ford admired the pawnshop owner's ability to handle both a cigar and weed.

"Miss Bethany came here to surprise my Grace," Al said, handing her back the joint. "Brought my nephew along with her."

"You work for Al?" Bethany asked.

"God help it if you think I'd smoke a doobie in front of an employee," Al said. "Sparrow here's painting Grace."

"I do collage work," Ford clarified.

"Oh, you're *Ford!*" she said, having evidently missed his previous introduction. She studied him from across the fire, trying to see what hid behind his costume's hair extensions.

"Grace mentioned the collage," Bethany said.

"Is she not here?" Ford asked.

"Her and my nephew are up there acting like children," Al said, pointing indiscriminately at the house. "Happy couple that they are."

Ford eyed the broken bottleneck, which Bethany still held. He knew Grace was married. He had known when they kissed on the parkway. He'd hoped as their lips touched she'd see it wasn't so difficult a decision. But the yellow Mitsubishi kept her from truly finding out. They hadn't seen or spoken to each other since. When the invitation arrived for the Halloween party, Ford wondered if she'd mailed it out prior to their drive. He hadn't bothered to ask. Afraid if he did, she wouldn't respond and that'd be his answer.

Bethany tossed the bottleneck over the balcony.

Al laughed. "I swear young lady if you weren't married, I'd marry you right now." He turned to Ford. "You believe a woman this beautiful is a mother of three?"

Ford didn't care. But he tried. Aware that Al was testing him in some way. Aware that Bethany was doing the same. So he nodded.

"Yes ma'am, you and my niece are by far the prettiest girls I've ever seen." Al's eyes locked in on the flames. "And for that nephew of mine to piss it all away."

"Not in good company, dear," Bethany said.

14

"Oh, you break my heart calling me *dear* like that. Meredith called me dear." Al drew on his cigar. "You married, Sparrow?"

"I—"

"Meredith was the one that got away," he said, interrupting Ford. "Mark me a damn fool. You got children, Sparrow?"

"No," Ford lied.

"You got siblings that do?"

"No," he continued to lie.

"You got siblings, I assume," Al said, impatient with all of Ford's noes.

"Yes," Ford conceded.

"Good," Al said. "'Cause here's some advice, free of charge." The fire reflected in Al's eyes. "Have kids before they do. Forget them before they forget you."

"Well, you've certainly taken a turn," Bethany said. "He's usually very charming," she told Ford.

"Tired!" Al shouted. "Certainly tired of not knowing. Tell me—did he or did he not hit that woman? And who the hell was she anyway?"

"We're in good company," Bethany said, smiling stiffly at Ford.

"I should go," Ford said, standing.

"No, sit down," Al commanded.

"Ford, let's go find Grace," Bethany suggested.

"Oh, I see," Al said. "I've said too much."

Bethany leaned in front of Al, tilting back his cowboy hat and kissing him on the forehead. "You can't be sensitive *and* mean. Not all at once. I'll come back after I find Gracie."

Al smiled. "I swear I'd marry you, Miss Bethany."

"I bet you would," she said. "But you and I both know it'd never be as good as we have it right here."

Upstairs, bookshelves lined three of the four walls. Bethany sat on the leather couch perpendicular to the room's large oak desk. She tucked her feet beneath her legs and ran her fingers through her blonde wig.

Ford remained standing, scanning the titles. Each shelf was organized by author or subject matter: American cinema, the Civil War, Shakespeare, Nazi Germany, local history, Agatha Christie, baseball, NASCAR, George Washington, Abraham Lincoln, Theodore Roosevelt, world religions, antiques, memorabilia, self-help, classic automobiles, Mark Twain, the mafia, Thomas Wolfe, Wilma Dykeman, O. Henry, Rudyard Kipling and an entire two shelves dedicated to astronomy.

"Quite the variety," Ford exclaimed, still admiring the collection.

"When he's not losing his shit he's actually a pretty interesting guy to talk to," Bethany said.

Ford turned around. "What was that all about anyway?" he asked.

She studied him. "Don't worry about it."

Ford didn't press, knowing she would relay such demands to Grace. Bethany continued to consider him. He wasn't sure where to look. He wasn't sure what to think either. Why were they here? Was she hiding him from the husband? Would he ever get to see Grace tonight? Did she even want to see him? Had the whole thing been a mistake?

He glanced at Bethany. "Who are you supposed to be?" he asked, just to say something.

"Roxie Hart," she said incredulously. "From *Chicago*. Gracie's Velma Kelly. JR didn't want to play along." She laughed. "So now we've got two Jack Sparrows."

He considered her final comment. "Should I not be here?" he asked.

Bethany smiled. "You're the whole reason we're having this party," she said. "JR's the one who isn't supposed to be here. But once he found out I was flying in, there was no stopping him. He thinks I'm a bad influence. Because I speak my mind. The Burnett men do not care for women who speak their minds."

Her words were reassuring. As if sensing his relief, Bethany patted the cushion next to her. Ford accepted the invitation. Again, she briefly studied him before grabbing a throw pillow and hugging it against her chest.

"Gracie tells me you're divorced."

The comment was jarring, but Ford quickly recovered. All that it meant was that Grace had been talking about him to Bethany. This was a good thing.

"Ten years now," Ford said.

Speaking the words aloud made it difficult to fathom. Ten years meant he and Emily had been divorced now for a longer period than they'd been married. He'd spent the first five years getting over the whole thing and then another two years before he could readily acknowledge the previous five. And now, three years later and ten years apart, it was hard to imagine where all that time had gone.

"And you've got a son?" Bethany asked, continuing her line of questioning.

Ford nodded. "He'll be eighteen in December."

Bethany reached over and grabbed Ford's wrist. "December what?"

"Sixteenth," he answered, surprised by her question's urgency.

"Oh," she said, releasing him. "Mine's the ninth."

He didn't know why but her disappointment amused him. The laughter came from deep within his belly, eventually watering his eyes. Ford's bout triggered Bethany's own. And so the two strangers laughed together on a couch inside another stranger's private study.

"I'm supposed to fly out there to celebrate with him," Ford said, wiping away the tears. "He lives in Los Angeles with his mother. I still haven't booked a flight."

The confession embarrassed him. But Bethany wasn't listening. Her laughter had ceased. She sat there with stiff shoulders and eyes fixed on the bookshelves. Her brief trance concluded with a deep sigh. She then surprised Ford by unloading her own marital problems. She recently discovered that her husband had been cheating on her with the nanny. At one point, Ford couldn't tell if Bethany was more upset by her husband's betrayal or his conventional approach to an affair.

"I still love him, though," she said. "Even when I hate myself for it. And it's not like sleeping with you would change any of that."

Her remark made sex sound like a foregone conclusion. The assumption offended Ford, yet the idea itself was intriguing.

"I decided that outside on the porch," she continued. "If anything, sleeping with you would only make me angrier. Of course, Gracie's hoping I will because she thinks if I do it'll somehow wear off the spell you've got her under."

Bethany shook her head fiercely. "I talk too much when I'm stoned," she said. "It gets me in trouble."

Ford wasn't sure if she was genuinely distressed or quietly requesting that he pry. He considered Bethany's profile a moment longer.

"What's Grace's situation?" he asked.

She exhaled loudly. "Don't ask."

"But I did."

She turned to him with heavy, cynical eyes. "I'm very stoned," she said. "And you're taking advantage. I'm not sure how I feel about this."

Ford didn't respond. He could see she was deciding. His words would only delay things.

"You can't tell her I told," she said.

He nodded.

"I'm serious."

He nodded again.

In high school, Grace and JR had a friend named George Peterson, Bethany told Ford. For a period the three were inseparable. But George left Houston his senior year. Shortly after his departure, Bethany began overhearing one-sided phone conversations between her mother and her mother's friends.

First it went that George was institutionalized. Then that he was in treatment for drugs. Then: *have you spoken with Janet? ... You have to call her. ... Well, of course I'm going tell you. ... He isn't in Wyoming and he isn't in the hospital. He's in Austin, with—are you ready for this? A man. ... Yes, I'm certain. ... Call Janet if you don't believe me. ... I know, I know, I know. Poor Barbara and Stan. ... Well, of course it's embarrassing. It's disgusting. He had all the advantages. And for him to go and do something like this. It's appalling. ...*

Once the topic of George's sexuality was exhausted, his name was dropped from all adult conversations. As far as Bethany's mother and her mother's friends were concerned, he no longer existed. An unwanted fuckup not worth remembering because it didn't make any sense: how parents— good parents—like Barbara and Stan Peterson could create something like that. No, it wasn't worth the energy.

Until, that is, George returned to Houston by way of Montreal by way of Portland by way of San Francisco. A decade gone, he came back a changed man.

"He'd been a beautiful boy," Bethany told Ford. "So it makes sense that he'd make a beautiful woman. He's got those

20

high anorexic looking cheekbones and big, beautiful blue eyes. How he got that ass, I have no idea. Still, it's not like we didn't know. And it's not like George was hiding it."

Bethany removed the blonde wing, surprising Ford with her blonde hair beneath it. She scratched at her scalp before placing the wing back on.

"She goes by Georgia now," Bethany continued, adjusting the hairpiece. "And JR was spotted with Georgia at a bar out in Sugar Land. *Twice.* We're talking away from the city. Nobody goes to Sugar Land for a drink. Unless you're hiding something. Of course, JR insists that he wasn't hiding anything. But this is all secondhand. Not that that makes it any less true. Plus, once the rumors did spread, Georgia ended up with a black eye and a broken nose. I *saw* those. And that's when talk really started. JR gets spotted with Georgia, rumor spreads, and a week later Georgia has a broken face. And then a few days after that JR has the outburst on-air. He must have yelled *faggot* fifty times."

She considered her next point.

"You don't break a person's face over false accusations," she said. "You break a person's face over genuine hurt. I nearly broke my husband's face after I found the pictures on his phone. I mean can you believe that? Why would you keep pictures on your phone? Our kids could have seen those. That fucking idiot. I should have broken his face."

She took a deep breath.

"JR's parents shipped him to Dallas after he got fired," she continued. "He apparently had a nervous breakdown. But the story the Burnetts are telling is that Gracie and JR are up here helping with Uncle Al's businesses. They're claiming Al had a stroke."

Bethany chewed on the side of her thumbnail. The floor began to vibrate. She stood. "The DJ's here," she exclaimed. "Let's go dance."

"What about Grace?" Ford asked.

"They're fighting," she said. "She'll find us when she finds us."

Bethany pulled Ford toward the door. She paused before opening it. "Would you kiss me?" she asked.

There was no presumption in her request. She couldn't even look him in the eyes. It surprised Ford. Every last bit of it. Not least, his sudden desire to hold this stranger and cry.

"But nothing else," she insisted, her eyes meeting his. "I can't go home without some sort of guilt. I'm trying to forgive my husband."

Ford kissed her. Out of spite. And resentment. And jealousy. A petty kiss. A kiss given knowing somewhere in the house Grace fought with another man. Her husband.

Bethany quickly broke away. Nervous, she playfully tapped his nose. "Let's go dance, Jack Sparrow."


Lenny stumbled toward them. "Captain Hook," he called out.

Ford introduced him to Bethany. Bethany turned to Ford and stated the obvious: "Your friend is very drunk."

The red paint circling Lenny's lips ran down the white paint of his beard. He rested a heavy hand on Ford's shoulder, panting.

"Bethany needs a dance partner," Ford told him.

Lenny's eyelids barely held open. Bethany again repeated the fact that he was very drunk. Ford insisted Lenny was anemic. Bethany disappeared into the crowd.

The drunk clown turned toward the dance floor, pointing. His finger rose and fell in the air as if he was tracing the movement of a housefly. Then suddenly his hand dropped.

"Air," Lenny barked, leaning heavier on Ford's shoulder.

On the front porch, Lenny collapsed, laughing. The laughter carried a hint of self-consciousness. As if Lenny knew he was drunk and he knew he had fallen, but he wanted Ford to know that he wasn't *that* drunk and certainly not *that* fallen.

Still, Lenny didn't bother trying to stand. Instead, he spun on his side in a slow counterclockwise motion. "Couldn't find you, brother," he said, still spinning.

"You're gonna hurt yourself."

"Couldn't find you," Lenny repeated. "Figured you was gone. Figured I was left to fend for myself. Figured I was stranded here on Pinchot Creek Mountain."

"Well, here I am."

"And there you are," Lenny agreed sharply. "And here I am, spinning like a damn fool."

Lenny paused, staring up at Ford, his eyes glazed over and far away. "You ever get the feeling like nothing's quite how it's supposed to be?"

"Sometimes," Ford said.

Lenny grinned. "Not me, brother. Down here everything's ga-roo-vy." His arms and legs then went limp. His eyes closed. His heavy breath billowed out from his nose.

In the front yard, between a pair of oaks, Grace emerged. Her appearance was surreal in that she was clearly laughing, but Ford could not hear it. She continued toward the house, her hand resting across her stomach. For a moment, Ford imagined that she wasn't laughing but crying, her arm concealing a wound. But as she neared, her laughter broke through the crisp air. Her shoulders, covered by a fur coat, convulsed.

"Always, always, always the last place you look," she said.

"Where'd you come from?"

Grace paused at the bottom of the front porch steps, counting and recounting them as if one had gone missing. "Out walking after midnight," she said.

"It's not midnight."

She looked at her wrist, despite not wearing a watch. "Guess not."

On the porch she pressed into Ford. "It's cold."

He rubbed the soft sleeves of her coat.

"Is that Lenny?" she asked, pointing at the clown.

Ford nodded.

"Is he dead?"

"Just practicing."

She leaned over and playfully tapped Lenny on his forehead. When he didn't respond, she honked the rubber nose that dangled below his beard.

24

Lenny groaned.

Grace stood upright. "I lost my wig," she said, looking out onto the property. "Lost it somewhere out there."

She faced Ford, opening her coat to show off her costume: a dazzling black dress. "I'm Velma Kelly from *Chicago*." She closed the coat. "But I lost my wig," she repeated, pointing toward the darkness. "The valet guy's out there looking for it. God, I'm such a bitch."

Then, as if seeing Ford for the first time, she covered her mouth. "No!" she said, shaking her head. "Are you kidding?"

He waited for an explanation.

"Tell me you aren't Jack Sparrow."

"I'm not Jack Sparrow."

"Yes you are!"

"I'm Captain Hook," he claimed.

She grabbed his hands. "You don't have a hook," she said. "You *are* Jack Sparrow."

Grace led Ford off the porch and down the gravel walkway. As they neared the woods, the valet driver appeared from within the cluster of oaks and pines.

"I looked everywhere," he told Grace. "Are you sure you lost it out there?"

"It's fine," Grace insisted. "We'll find it."

"You want my flashlight," he called after them.

She ignored the offer.

The two entered the woods in silence. As they stepped farther into the darkness their hands locked. They came to a clearing. Chairs surrounded an empty fire pit. She directed him to sit and then lowered herself onto his lap.

"It's too cold not to share," she told him.

"I met Bethany," Ford said.

"I'm very upset with her."

"She seems nice enough," he said.

"Don't play dumb."

They were both silent. He studied her in the darkness, unable to gauge her expression.

"Well, where is he then?" Ford asked.

"Upstairs, probably."

He placed his hands over Grace's laced arms.

"I haven't stopped thinking about you," she said. "Even with him here. I was so shocked to see him. And then I felt guilty. But he's so unbearable. But I don't know if it's just because I want him to be that way. I don't know if it's all in my head. But then I don't know if I care either way. I've been waiting for this all week. And then he showed up. I should have told you. But I wanted you to come tonight."

"Does he know?"

"He wouldn't care either way."

"So then he knows."

"We haven't done anything," she said. "Not really."

"But you wanted me to come here tonight."

"I missed you."

They kissed. He could taste the vodka on her tongue. Ford ran his hands across the midsection of her dress.

"Am I a bad person?" she asked.

He continued to kiss her neck.

"It's very dark out here," she said.

His lips traveled across her clavicle.

"And I'm Velma Kelly and you're Jack Sparrow."

"Captain Hook," Ford said.

"No," she insisted. "Jack Sparrow."

His hands continued to explore her. She kissed him once more, unbuckling his belt.

"Are you cold?" she whispered.

"No," he said.

"Me neither."

She removed her coat. He went to take off his hat.

"Leave it," she said.

"You're shaking."

"I'm fine," she said, pulling the top half of her dress down toward her waist before putting back on her coat. She placed his hands on her breasts and they kissed beneath the tall oaks. The cold air raised her skin. Her ribs quivered. She sank her teeth into his bottom lip. He tasted salt and thought of the ocean. Her teeth released him.

"Did you miss me?" she asked.

"Of course," he said.

Her bones continued to rattle as she hiked up the lower half of her dress. She struggled to remove her underwear. He went to help, but she wouldn't let him. He worked on his zipper instead.

"Do you remember what you said to me at the Grove Park?" she asked, once they were both undone.

His hands inched up her legs. "We said a lot of things," he reminded her.

"Just before we went to Fitzgerald's room," she said.

He could hear it in her voice. Forgetting was not an option.

"Do you remember?" she repeated.

"Yes," he lied.

"Say it again," she said.

He didn't panic. That was the only reason he remembered.

"I said you were the easiest person to talk to."

"Did you mean it?" she asked.

"I did," he said.

And this was the truth.

# CHAPTER 2

Monday morning. Ford sat alone inside his studio. Lenny stayed home, still recovering from Saturday night. Their shared space was located on the second floor of a former industrial building originally constructed in the 1880s as part of the old lumberyard. At one point, in the 1970s, it functioned as an air conditioning factory. Then it sat vacant, used only by junkies. Eventually, the junkies got booted by the artists. And more recently some of the downstairs artists got booted by the new owner, who needed a spot for his son's wine bar. (The kid knew nothing about wine, but it gave him something to do.)

Despite these recent changes, Lumberyard Studios still housed eighteen artists between its two levels. But the rumors never ended. Rent was going to double, then triple, within the next six months. Evictions were imminent. The owner's son planned to expand his space into a full-fledged restaurant and put condos upstairs.

Two years into the new ownership, Ford quit paying attention. His rent had increased fifteen percent. Otherwise, he and Lenny still had the same setup they'd started with three and a half years ago: eight hundred square feet divided into an open gallery up front, two private studios in the back, and a kitchenette off to the side. The space overlooked the train tracks and beyond that the river.

Most of Ford's works were visual interpretations of songs. But for his son's birthday he wanted to try something different. He wanted to capture all sixteen tracks of Arcade Fire's *The Suburbs* in a single image.

Ford played the album on his laptop. A crash cymbal introduced its opening title track. The song devastated Ford, as did most of *The Suburbs*. The entire album seemed built around the notion that youth was not wasted on the young, but that youth *was* waste. And most of the lyrics suggested a desire to return to the waste. But by album's end, as the opening song's chorus was repeated as the final line, the nostalgia turned in on itself, revealing that the album's true loss was not the past but the desire to desire the past. *The Suburbs* was an album nostalgic for the lost sense of nostalgia.

"I said, excuse me!"

Like most proud men, Ford did not appreciate being startled. The responsible party stood in the doorway with his arms crossed, hands hugging opposite elbows. He was half a foot taller than Ford, easily six-foot-six. Ford remained silent with clenched fists.

"I'd been calling from the front for some time," the man said, managing to sound both apologetic and annoyed.

"There's usually two of us here," Ford told him.

"I could have robbed the place," the man said, as if the act itself would have been Ford's fault.

"Well, I appreciate your self-control."

The man looked him over. "Are you Ford Carson?"

Ford tried placing the man. He had a thin nose, a pronounced jawline, and ears that were far too small for his head. His hair, kept short on the sides, was parted on the left with a thick brown wave flowing toward the right. The true extent of his build was concealed behind a black coat. Nevertheless, something in the way he carried himself suggested a former athlete. Perhaps it was the stiffness of his shoulders and neck.

"You know my wife," the man continued. His tone wasn't accusatory so much as factual. "I'm JR Burnett."

Ford didn't panic. He'd learned long ago how to divide himself in stressful situations. The one good thing to come out of his divorce. Granted, it was a slow lesson coming. But he had it now. And so he briefly stepped outside of himself to observe the situation for what it was: a husband confronting his wife's lover.

"Good to meet you," Ford said.

JR scratched between his eyebrows with his pinky nail, scraping at the flesh as if picking at an invisible scab. "I assume you had a good time the other night," he said, examining his nail. He studied it a moment longer before looking over at Ford. "Well?" he asked impatiently. "Did you enjoy the party or not?"

Ford knew he had no reason to dislike this man outside of the fact that he very much liked this man's wife and wanted to continue to like her without the sort of interference and trouble this man posed.

"It had its moments," Ford said. "Can I get you a coffee?" he asked, walking past JR. It felt good to leave the confines of his studio.

"No, I'm fine," JR said, following closely behind.

Ford bypassed the kitchenette, positioning himself behind the gallery's front counter. "Well, what can I do for you—BJ was it?"

JR corrected Ford, adding, "It's short for Jeffrey."

"What about the *R*?"

"What about it?" JR asked, circling the front of the gallery, his hands deep inside his coat pockets.

Ford remained behind the counter, calm but anticipatory.

"I suppose there are two options for every woman," JR said, still walking about the room. He let the statement linger for a moment. He then turned about-face, pausing, his hands locked behind his back. "They either marry their father or carry out an affair with him."

Ford nearly laughed. The lines had clearly been rehearsed and JR Burnett was no actor. No writer either.

"That's an interesting theory," Ford said. "Is Grace's father tall?"

"Is her father tall?" JR asked, perplexed.

"Like you," Ford said.

"No, he's not tall." JR shook his head briskly. "He's dead."

"Are all dead men short?" Ford asked.

JR stared at him quizzically. "I understand you and my wife have become friends," he said. "And just so you know, I'm using that as a euphemism. I realize the two of you are fucking."

The blunt declaration shook Ford. Not because of JR's knowledge but rather because of the constant variation in his tone.

JR approached the counter, rapping his fingers swiftly against it. "She's not well, you know." He said it in a way that sounded conspiratorial. As if he was letting Ford in on a secret. A secret he wanted Ford to recognize as such so that JR might, on a later date, refer back to this initial exchange as an act of goodwill.

Ford took a moment to respond.

"She seemed fine at the party."

"That's because you don't know her," JR said. "Not like I do."

Ford saw no reason to debate this point.

"Listen," JR said, pausing to adjust his jaw with his index finger and thumb. He then ran his fingers through his hair. "I think I'll take that coffee after all."

Inside the kitchenette, Ford eyed the knife block. He shifted his head to keep track of his visitor but discovered he was alone. He listened. The front gallery was silent. He listened some more. For anything. A breath. A footstep. A sigh.

The door's threshold took on the threat of a guillotine. Ford approached it cautiously, nearly leaping to the other side.

JR sat on the gallery's old leather couch, his elbows on his knees, his forehead in his hands.

Ford cleared his throat, startling his distraught guest.

"Where's the coffee?" JR demanded.

"How do you take it?" Ford asked.

"Take it?"

"Sugar? Cream?"

JR exhaled. "Both," he said sharply. Then with a gentler tone, he added: "Please."

Ford retreated.

"No," JR barked. "Just sugar. Or you know what? Fuck it. Black. Just give it to me black."

Ford returned with a cup of black coffee.

"You're not having any?" JR asked.

"I've had plenty."

JR studied the mug with a look suspicious of poisoning.

"You don't have an end table," he finally said.

"No one usually sits here," Ford answered.

"Why do you have a couch then?"

"In case people wanted to sit here."

"You need an end table," JR informed him. "What am I supposed to do with this mug? How am I supposed to relax? How are *you* supposed to relax?"

"I can bring a crate from the back."

"I saw your look," JR said. "You're scared. Just like everyone else."

Ford half-anticipated JR hurling the coffee at his face. Instead, JR placed the mug on the ground and slid it beneath the couch.

"They've classified me unstable," JR said, leaning back. "I never thought of myself as unstable. Not until they started pointing out all the unstable things I do. And so now I've got this bothersome crutch of a label, in that when I start acting a certain way I can't help but just assume it's because I'm in fact unstable."

Ford couldn't tell if this was a confession or a threat.

"You artists are supposed to be an unstable bunch," JR continued. "But then so are dentists. And even though they don't include lawyers in the mix, every last one I've met is a little off. Firefighters, soldiers, teachers, accountants—they're all unstable too. So really who does that leave us with?"

JR didn't wait for a response.

"The dead," he answered. "But you've got to be crazy to want to join that group. Although we will. And that's really the thought that shakes things up if you think about it for too long. My problem is I think about a lot of things too long. And I think a lot about what other people think and what makes it even worse is I care just as much. And I care even more about what they say. Even though we all know none of it means anything. But somehow we've convinced ourselves that it does. And *that's* the real problem."

JR paused, rolling his head to the side to see if Ford had anything to add. Ford remained silent, trying to separate himself from the situation again but without success.

"Where do you fall in with your family?" JR asked.

Ford didn't want to talk to this man about his family.

"The youngest? The oldest?" JR considered Ford for a moment. "You don't strike me as a middle child."

"Oldest," Ford said.

"How many siblings?"

"A sister."

"I'm the youngest of five. Three brothers, a sister, and me. Can you believe that? You'd have thought they'd've stopped after Justine. After they got the girl they'd been trying for. But they kept going. That's always thrown me. Not that they don't have the means. They could have had six more of us and they still wouldn't know what to do with all that money."

Once more JR adjusted his jaw, locking it back into place with his index finger and thumb. He glared at Ford, his eyes narrowing with disgust. "You don't give a shit," he said. "I'm rambling. I fucking ramble."

JR looked up toward the ceiling with a tight grin. His eyelids flickered. He leaned back into the couch.

"Grace and I love each other," he said. "I want you to know that. And if this is what she needs right now, I'm okay with it. But don't think this is anything more than what it is. You're her fuck-buddy, okay?"

Ford didn't respond.

"Do you understand me?" JR asked.

Ford nodded dully.

"How about you say *yes*, instead of nodding your dumb fucking head?"

Ford's phone rang. His ex-wife's name flashed across the screen.

"Who is it?" JR asked.

Ford could hear it in JR's voice. He was jealous. He thought it was Grace.

"Don't worry about it," Ford said, muting the call.

JR eyed the phone. Ford enjoyed his uncertainty.

"Are you close with your son?" JR asked.

Ford stood. "You can go now."

JR grinned. "But I still have my coffee," he protested, reaching for the mug.

"Enjoy your coffee then," Ford said, heading back to his studio.

"I could have stolen something, you know?" JR called after him. "When I first got here. You really ought to be more attentive."

"Go ahead," Ford said, his back still toward him.

"No, I don't think so."

Ford turned around. "Why not?"

"Because I don't need to steal," JR said. "I was just pointing it out."

"Right," Ford said. "You came all this way to point out that you *could* steal from me. And, of course, you *can*. So why not just do it?"

"That's not why I came here."

"That's right," Ford said, continuing their game of chess. "I forgot. You came here to tell me that I'm fucking your wife. And that that's all I'm doing."

"Correct," JR said.

"And now I'm telling you to steal something."

"No," JR insisted.

"But I told you to."

"I won't do it," JR said defiantly.

"Good," Ford said. "I'm glad you and I understand each other."


His phone rang again shortly after JR's departure. Emily's persistence annoyed him. But he also appreciated his ex-wife's doggedness. Her call prevented him from contacting Grace. Which was good. He didn't need to speak with her just yet. What would he have said anyway? *So I met your husband.* Or, *JR swung by the studio today.* Or, *How'd your husband know where I work?* Or, *How does your husband know who I am?* Or, *What the fuck?*

"I was just calling you back," Ford lied.

Emily was silent.

"You there?" he asked.

"Ford?" she responded, her voice fading in and out.

"You there?" he repeated.

"I can hear you," she said.

He waited.

"You there?" she asked.

"Yes," he said, impatient with all their nonstarters. "I was letting you talk."

They were both silent.

"I hadn't heard back from you," she said.

"I was just calling you back," he repeated his original lie.

"No," she said. "My email."

"What email?"

"I sent it three days ago."

"Did you send it to my personal or to the studio?"

"Both."

Ford vaguely remembered. He'd seen it on his phone but then forgot to read it. He tried explaining some version of this to Emily. She let it pass without comment. In the evolution of their post-marriage relationship this was her way of telling him to fuck off. Ten years divorced, neither could explicitly tell the other to fuck off without losing face. Sometimes Ford missed it. Civility was so sterile.

"Bailey wants to come to you," she said.

"What does that mean?"

"For his birthday," Emily explained. "He'd rather go there than you come here."

"Bailey wants to come *here*?"

"You're opposed to this?" she asked. "I thought if anything it'd be more convenient. We realize it's not easy for you to just drop everything."

Ten years, but she could still jab in subtle ways. Sometimes it was as if she couldn't help it. Maybe even missed it.

"The last time I went out there I hardly got to see him," Ford reminded her.

"He was competing," she reminded him back. "And you were here for two days."

"Four," he corrected her.

There was pause on her end. "It'd be nice," she finally said. "For your son to see where his father lives."

"I send him pictures all the time. He never responds."

"He's seventeen," Emily said.

They were both silent.

"I just don't want it to be a chore," Ford said.

She exhaled.

"And what about you?" he asked, pacing around his small studio. "You're gonna miss his eighteenth birthday?"

"We'll celebrate before he leaves."

Her accommodations made Ford uneasy. He continued to pace. "He'll resent me for it," he said. "Claim I kept him from being with his friends."

"He has no friends."

Ford stopped in his tracks. "So then who are all these people he's surfing the world with?"

"Those are kids he competes against," she said. "Nobody local. He hasn't changed, your son. Everyone here is just like everyone back in Cocoa Beach. If they're not up to his level, he assumes they're beneath him. If they are up to his level, he resents sharing the spotlight. He's a borderline narcissist."

"I wonder how that happened."

"Don't start."

Timothy Warwick, Emily's second husband, always struck Ford as the type of guy who laughed out loud while reading in public. She and Timothy got together shortly after she and Ford split. Ford remembered getting the news. Emily must have stopped herself ten times to repeat the fact that she was only telling Ford for Bailey's sake. That it was none of Ford's business otherwise. But that she didn't want Bailey to feel like he had to keep secrets from his dad.

Timothy was a lawyer. He and Ford were formally introduced at one of Bailey's surfing competitions in Cocoa Beach, Florida. Timothy had these watery blue eyes, half-concealed by droopy eyelids that looked like coagulated wax.

Timothy didn't cheer much that first day. A couple nervous claps at most. But over the ensuing months he grew comfortable. Until finally his support found voice. Once it did, Ford spent most of his son's competitions watching this strange man shout his boy's name. A shark's upper jaw isn't fused to its head; that's what allows it to open its mouth so wide. And that's what Ford pictured every time Timothy cheered. He looked like a shark devouring some invisible prey.

Early on, Ford tried not to pry into his ex-wife's new life. But on certain nights, when the headlines read dull and the commercials kept rolling and he'd scrolled past every desperate status update from every desperate old high school pal, he'd succumb.

At first the spying reassured him. On Emily's feed there was no mention of her new shark-jawed beau. Clearly, they weren't serious. But Shark Man's absence soon made Ford uneasy. What if, unlike all the others trying to post their lives into meaningful existence, Emily and Shark Man didn't need the sort of desperate online confirmation?

Ford's fear was briefly mitigated once Shark Man did start appearing. Clearly, they were miserable. Who else shares an entire album of bowling alley pictures?

But before long a new problem emerged: Ford couldn't put Shark Man away. He tried laughing off most of what he discovered. Shark Man was not merely an attorney but also the shoeless front man of an acoustic, middle-aged, three-piece rock band called New Day Rising. Ford acted (for his own private benefit) like it was an accident when he clicked the link to New Day Rising's Myspace page. Pictures appeared that he hadn't anticipated. Emily and Bailey off to the right of a small coffee shop stage, smiling as New Day Rising performed its latest set. All the while, Shark Man's vocals came through Ford's computer speakers in pants and moans—a shameless albeit failed attempt to sound like Bono. His lyrics were what drove Ford to close out of the site . . . *your beauty like a rose, sweet darling / your soft petals, my milky way.*

"He'll be eighteen," Emily said over the phone. "After this, who knows? You should take him while you can. While either one of us can still pretend to have any say."

Ford nearly asked how she'd handle the empty nest, having momentarily forgotten there were now two others that he knew very little about. Bailey's half-siblings. He'd only met them a half-dozen times.

"His birthday falls on a Wednesday," Emily said. "I don't supposed you'd want to keep him through the holidays."

They agreed on the dates. Five days. Afterward, Ford mentioned that he was working on a piece for Bailey's birthday. Emily sounded genuinely surprised.

"You know I show him all the articles they've written about you," she said.

Ford gazed at his son's blank canvas. "I'm sure he reads them with vigor and pride."

"He's seventeen," she said. "He's an asshole to everyone."


Ford tried immersing himself back into *The Suburbs*. The more he listened the heavier the project became. He wanted to come at it from Bailey's perspective. He wanted to capture an image that would resonate with his son's sensibility. He wanted to forget the fact that he was Bailey's father because he knew it would impede the work. Which it did. Because he *was* Bailey's father. And that's what this would be. Bailey would arrive expecting a new iPhone or a couple hundred bucks. Not a collage. Although another part of Ford imagined otherwise. Like every father in the world he wanted to impress his son.

Ford turned off *The Suburbs*.

Outside his studio, the gallery was still. JR's coffee mug remained beneath the couch. Ford took out his phone and texted Grace. He wrote her: *Did you ever end up finding your wig?*

# CHAPTER 3

Ford first met Grace on his birthday. His plan had been to observe the day alone at the Grove Park Inn. He liked its history—the stone structure was over a hundred years old. And he liked its ambiance—there was something strange and lonely about the place. But above all, he liked its whiskey—he could sit with it alone inside the inn's Great Hall without the shame he felt whenever he did the same thing at his favorite dive down the road.

Earlier that day, Emily had called to wish him a happy fortieth. In their ten years apart she'd never bothered with such niceties. It made him uneasy. He thought maybe she had cancer. Then he worried Bailey had cancer. Then he thought: I deserve cancer.

It turned out no one had cancer. Rather, Emily used the occasion to see about Ford coming west for Bailey's eighteenth birthday. The request caught him off guard, which immediately embarrassed him. He should have been the one initiating such plans.

Emily invited Ford to stay at the Warwick household. Ford stammered. Despite feeling nauseated, he told Emily sure. She sounded pleased, as if she actually wanted him there. The nausea lasted long after their conversation. In fact, it continued until his first drink inside the Great Hall. Only then did he realize that this was the beginning of the end. Bailey was turning eighteen. After that, Ford and Emily would have no need for each other. No obligation to check in.

Her invitation was a declaration of independence, Ford decided. His final guest appearance before he became just a name. *How has your father been?* she might ask Bailey during some future holiday. And Bailey would shrug and that would be as far as the conversation went.

Suicide crossed Ford's mind. An old thought. He knew he wouldn't. Certainly not because of this. But the idea lingered. A few drinks, a warm bath, and a sharp razor could end it all.

Ford was still considering his death when he spotted Grace. She stood before one of the Great Hall's two stone fireplaces. During the colder months the staff built giant log fires. But in late August the wood stretched across the andirons as mere decoration.

Her hair mesmerized Ford. He'd never seen strands so black. Grace turned as if sensing his attention from the bar. Her eyelids narrowed with suspicion. He mirrored her expression, aware only then of the conceit that accompanies those experiencing unshakeable gloom—a sense that no one has suffered quite like you until you recognize it in someone else.

She stepped out onto the terrace. The late lunch crowd had died down. Only a few remained outside with their cappuccinos and cocktails. Ford watched Grace through the window. She stood before the stone steps that led down to the spa, her focus on the distant mountains. The view must have kept her from noticing the wren as it flew in from the golf course. Ford watched the bird tuck in its wings before it crashed into the side of Grace's head. Both woman and bird went down.

"Are you okay?" Ford asked, joining her outside.

Grace massaged her scalp. Next to her the injured wren twitched. A few feet away, a father and son sat oblivious to it all. The father thumbed away on his phone while the boy speared cherries with his black straw.

"Would you please?" Grace asked, pointing at the damaged creature.

Ford didn't initially understand.

"It's suffering," she said.

Ford grabbed a napkin from the adjacent table. The father kept texting, but the boy took notice. He watched as this strange man placed the napkin—the very same cloth his father had just used to wipe his hands and mouth—over the small bird, crushing the creature with the back of his boot.

The boy ran off. Ford didn't bother notifying the father. Instead, he returned the napkin to the table with the flattened bird wrapped inside it.

Grace laughed. The man looked at her, annoyed, before realizing his son was gone. He shot up, scanning the terrace and calling out the boy's name.

"He's inside," Ford said, hating the man.

Once alone, he and Grace quietly considered each other. "I imagine you could probably use a drink," Ford said.

At the bar she ordered a lemon drop. Ford finished his glass of whiskey. Grace studied the place. Ford asked where she was visiting from.

"Houston," she said, looking past him toward the other fireplace. An older man sat reading in one of the rocking chairs.

Ford asked what she was in town for.

Her two index fingers circled the base of her glass. She did this three times. "My uncle," she began, before considering the rest of her response. "He lives in the area. I'm staying with him. He mentioned that Fitzgerald frequented this place back in the thirties. He's one of my favorites. I've got a soft spot for drunk assholes."

Ford was not a religious man. But between Grace's affinity for Fitzgerald and the dead bird that brought them together, he did briefly wonder if their meeting was preordained. "I've got his room," he said.

Grace did not respond with the enthusiasm he'd anticipated. Instead, she took a deliberate sip and considered his face. She needed to figure him out.

"Fitzgerald turned forty here," Ford continued.

Grace put down her glass. "He tried killing himself in that room."

"Yeah, but it didn't take."

She offered an opaque smile. The expression could have been amusement or disdain.

Ford distracted himself with his drink. He'd only recently read Fitzgerald's work. In general, he preferred biographies.

Mostly ones about musicians. But a client had commissioned him to do a collage based on *The Great Gatsby*. He read the book to figure out his entry into the project. And then he read books about the book to better understand it. And then he reread the book to fully grasp it.

Later on, he read up on Scott and Zelda. Their lifestyle frustrated him. They willed tragedies. But then tragic people often fascinated Ford. Or rather, knowing something tragic was going to happen and knowing the subject was completely unaware of its inevitably had a way of reassuring him. Like if he studied these accounts enough times, he might recognize the signs within his own life and avoid it.

"Are you a writer?" Grace asked.

Ford continued to peer into his whiskey. "Far from it," he said, digging through his pant pocket until he pulled out a business card. "I do mostly collage."

She looked it over. "Your studio's in Asheville," she said, confused.

Her confusion confused him.

"It is," he said.

"So then why the room here?"

Her confusion became less confusing.

"I thought it'd be interesting to turn forty where Fitzgerald did."

She raised her glass and wished him a happy birthday. He only had an ice cube left. She lowered her glass and ordered him another round. Ford tried to contest. But she called it bad luck to toast an ice cube. When his drink arrived, they did things right. He hadn't had dinner. The more they talked the more he kept wondering what they might look like together in Fitzgerald's room.

"You weren't planning to off yourself tonight, were you?"

"Excuse me?" he asked.

Her head snapped back with unrestrained laughter. "Sorry," she said. "I say dark things when I'm drunk."

Only then did he understand. "Oh, the room," he said, forcing a laugh. "No, I planned for just the nervous breakdown portion of Scott's stay. They have a whole list of options when you spend the night there."

"I'd love to see it."

"I'd be happy to show you, but I don't want you thinking I'm a creep."

"And I'd be happy to accept the invitation, but I wouldn't want you turning into a creep."

They had another round.

Her skin was flawless outside of a small scar just below her left cheekbone. Her teeth lined perfectly on top while the bottom row pressed and wedged against each other. Often after she spoke her tongue ran across her lower lip like she was catching leftover words.

"That's what I keep coming back to," she said. "It's like our roles switched or something. I mean my husband used to be the stable one. At least when we were dating. But we were just kids back then. Just stupid kids."

Ford realized he'd missed a good bit of what she'd been saying. Except for the word *husband*. He looked at her finger. No ring.

"Are you okay?" she asked.

He laughed as if that proved something. "I was just thinking," he said, pausing to locate a thought. "I haven't been here in five years. To this bar. Every year I end up somewhere else with someone I don't want to be with." He waved the comment off. "That isn't what this is. That's what that sounded like, I realize. I enjoy your company. Here, I mean. At this bar. We're strangers, I realize."

A smile touched the corners of her mouth. Ford got nervous. He continued rambling, trying to talk his way out of thinking too much. He was tired of meaningless sex. He didn't want to be that person. Not anymore. Those sad, lonely nights wasted with strangers. He was past all that now. Past that decade. What he needed was stability. Something a married woman like Grace could never be. And so he kept talking to avoid bleeding his thirties into his forties.

Ford's approach eventually led to the story of Bob and Virginia Smith. A story that should have scared Grace off. The very reason he told it. Ford hadn't thought about the Smiths in years. Which was odd, he realized, considering he still had a painting of their dead son hanging above his mantle.

Ford met the Smiths at the very same bar, he told Grace. Only then he had just turned thirty-five instead of forty and was new to the area, having left Florida a week prior, shortly after selling the family business.

The mountains, he convinced himself, would make him happy. His logic was based on sheer desperation. The source of his undiagnosed depression became geographical rather than psychological. And so naturally, leaving behind the hot flatlands of his home state would bring with it a new outlook, a new perspective, a new day.

Ford lived at the Grove Park Inn for nearly two weeks. He spent his mornings sipping coffee and staring out onto the mountains. During the afternoons he explored the trails. At night, he sat at the bar inside the Great Hall, buying rounds to ensure company for the duration of each drink.

Bob Smith liked gin. His wife, Virginia, liked gin too. The three ended up ordering rounds late into the evening. Bob did something in finance. Virginia spoke only of art. The latter was what brought the couple to Asheville. Specifically to buy an encaustic painting. Ford had never heard of the medium. Virginia tried to explain it. She laughed more than anything, repeating the fact that she couldn't do it. That he had to *see* it.

"Ford must come with us tomorrow," she insisted to her husband. She nodded at Ford compulsively. "You must." She returned to her husband. "Mustn't he?"

"Whatever you say," Bob told her, sipping his gin.

The next morning Ford sat on the Sunset Terrace, nursing a hangover. Fog drifted across the distant downtown. He heard his name. It took him a moment to recognize Virginia. She wore spandex leggings, a gray Cornell t-shirt, and a navy blue hat. She told him about her morning run around the golf course. Ford's head throbbed from the previous night.

"Can you still make it?" she asked.

He had forgotten about the art talk. But it didn't matter. He could hear it in her voice. If he declined she'd fold in on herself. He said yes. She blinked excessively.

They reconvened an hour later. Once again, he didn't initially recognize her. She wore a black, sleeveless button-up and a pair of white skinny jeans.

"Where's Bob?" Ford asked.

"Still in bed," she said.

Valet brought around her rental. She asked Ford to drive. They didn't talk much at first.

"I might get emotional," she said a few miles out. "Not that I need to tell you."

"That's fine," he said, grateful to be driving, to have the road as a distraction.

"Bob tries, but he's just not there yet," she went on. "He's all jokes and business. I can't tell you how relieved I was when you brought up your son last night."

She paused. "I didn't mean it like that," she said.

Ford tried to remember what he'd told her about Bailey. Instead, he remembered Bob going off about Andy Reid, the Kansas City Chief's head coach. But the details were fuzzy.

"I don't want this to come out wrong," she continued. "But it just gave me so much hope, the way you talked about it. I just thought, well maybe this'll rub off on Bob. But he's not there yet."

The GPS interjected. Ford tried remembering any part of the previous night's exchange. He turned left onto Joseph

Street. Their destination was on the right. The studio operated out of the building's main level. A café named Ground Floor occupied the basement. Ford parked alongside the road, pulling the emergency brake.

Virginia took a deep breath. "Danny," she began, cutting herself off.

Ford thought she'd forgotten his name. He nearly corrected her, but she grabbed his hand and said, "Ford, do you ever stop worrying?"

He didn't know what the question referenced, but he knew the answer she wanted to hear. "Eventually," he said.

Her grip tightened. "I still worry," she said. Her sharp laughter cut through the car. "Isn't that the strangest thing? I still wake up sometimes wondering if he's okay. Even after I realize there isn't anything else I could have done. Anything else I could do. But I still worry."

She looked at him for reassurance. He still didn't know what he was reassuring. But he comforted her anyway. "That's just how it is," he said.

She let go of his hand, nodding absently.


The artist, Jane Fellow, greeted them with an earnest smile and compassionate eyes. "You must be Bob," she said, leaning in for a hug.

"Ford," Virginia corrected her. "Bob's being Bob. Ford's an old friend."

The front half of the shop functioned as Jane's gallery. Canvases lined the walls with waves of colors forming ovals and clouds. Most were abstract. But some of the pieces incorporated recognizable elements: a telephone, a clock, a lampshade.

"I've got Danny's piece in the back," Jane said.

On hearing the name, Virginia collapsed into one of studio's red oval chairs. Jane hovered over her. Virginia insisted she was fine.

"Maybe some water?" Jane asked.

Virginia ignored her. "Aren't they fantastic?" she said to Ford, pointing listlessly at the wall.

Jane sat next to Virginia, rubbing her arm.

"They are," Ford agreed, using it as an excuse to turn away from the women.

A series of framed articles hung in a cluster near the front door. Jane's work garnered national attention, although state and local coverage accounted for a majority of the write-ups.

"What line of work are you in?" Jane asked Ford.

"Ford's an artist," Virginia answered for him. "Just like you."

Ford turned around. Had he claimed to be an artist the previous night? Virginia continued to stare off at the wall.

"Oh, lovely," Jane said with a tense smile. "What do you work in?"

Ford suddenly remembered Bob talking about a former business partner. The guy hanged himself a few years back, but the two were still friends on Facebook. Bob and Ford couldn't stop laughing. Bob kept repeating the word *Facebook* as if it was the punch line.

"I owned a printing company down in Dania Beach," Ford told Jane. "I just sold it."

Jane nodded.

"He creates these wonderful collages," Virginia said. "Show Jane the pictures you showed us last night."

Ford didn't remember showing Virginia his work. His first collage came about shortly after he and Emily split. Prior to that he'd primarily painted but only on occasion and in spurts.

The divorce brought about a restless energy. At first he wasted it, spending nights driving in and out of the Fort Lauderdale Airport. Security there never allowed anyone to stop. Which worked well for Ford, who just needed somebody to tell him to keep going. Driving in circles, he listened to Bruce Springsteen's *Nebraska*. He lived for that howl at the end of "State Trooper." Springsteen's cry had a way of reminding Ford that pain wasn't all that unique. The song wound up inspiring his first collage.

Jane flipped through Ford's phone, examining the photos without comment. Her silence made his skin burn. Why was he showing this woman his work?

"He creates them from songs," Virginia explained to Jane. Her tone had shifted. She was half-alive again. She took the phone from Jane, swiping frantically. "This one's my favorite. It's 'Jack and Diane.' The John Cougar song. Doesn't that take you back?"

"These are fantastic," Jane said.

To Ford's relief, Virginia handed him back his phone. "I think I'm ready," she told Jane.

A wide wooden table occupied the bulk of Jane's back studio. Atop it sat a series of trays with colors in both liquid and wax form, along with a blowtorch, hairdryer, and set of brushes. The table must have stood directly above the café's kitchen. Below them, pots clattered and music blasted.

Jane raised the bars of a drying rack and removed a canvas. Virginia gasped. "It's him," she said, covering her mouth. "It's my Danny."

Splashes of red, yellow, orange, and green accumulated into a wave, flowing toward but not quite reaching a lone tree. Ford didn't know what Virginia's boy looked like, but he assumed neither a wave nor a tree. (He'd later learn from Jane that Virginia's son had been at Cornell. Near the end of his freshman year he fell into one of the gorges. He planned to study botany, hence the tree.)

Virginia wiped the corner of her eye. "Do you do surfboards?" she asked Jane.

The question surprised Ford.

Virginia looked at him. "I thought maybe for your son."

"Your son surfs?" Jane asked.

Virginia frowned, reaching for Ford's hand. The gesture startled him. He pulled away. "I shouldn't have brought it up," she apologized, misinterpreting his response. She began to cry.

Ford's ears were on fire. He'd never had a high tolerance for tears. He'd learned a long time ago they didn't change anything.

"We're just so desperate, aren't we?" Virginia asked, once she regained control of her breathing. Her deep hollow laugh filled the room. She then collapsed but continued to howl. Jane hurried to her, but Virginia insisted she was fine.

Ford had every intention to leave, but Virginia got to him before he could withdraw. "How long ago did you say it was?" she asked.

"What are you talking about?"

"Oh, Ford," she said. "I thought you were different. *We can't all suffer alone.* That's what you said."

Ford had no idea what any of it meant. "You need to get up," he said.

"Don't change the subject." Virginia stood, leaning against the wall. "How the hell are you so calm?"

Downstairs a series of pots were thrown about.

"Virginia, everything's fine," Jane said.

"When did it happen?" Virginia demanded.

Both women faced Ford.

"I don't know what you're talking about," he said.

"Your son," Virginia screamed. She looked at Jane. "His boy drowned. Younger than my Danny. So how the hell is he so calm?"

Her words didn't initially register. Someone had turned the radio up downstairs. He could hear the chorus to the Traveling Wilburys' "End of the Line." He tapped his thumb against the side of his hip in step with the music.

"My boy didn't drown," he said, nodding his head to the tune.

"Is that how you sleep at night?" Virginia asked. "You're worse than Bob."

He couldn't stop listening to the music.

"His boy drowned," Virginia told Jane. "You should have heard the way he told it last night."

"Bailey's with his mother in L.A.," Ford said, his thumb still keeping beat.

"Ask Bob," she insisted, as if her husband waited in the next room.

Someone downstairs turned off the radio, ending the song abruptly.

"Why would I say that?" Ford asked. With the music gone, he lost his rhythm and felt defensive. "There's no reason I'd have said that."

Virginia stepped toward him on unstable legs. When Jane reached out to catch her, Virginia cringed as if she thought the support would sting. Still she let Jane hold her. When Virginia finally found her balance it looked like she might attack Ford. He half-welcomed it. But her body loosened while her eyes remained locked in on his. Her stare was neither sad nor scolding. In that moment it was as though she recognized something.

"You were just trying to be nice," she said.

Ford didn't know how to respond.

"You shouldn't say those sort of things," she continued. She took hold of his hands, digging her fingernails into his palms. "Don't say those things ever again."

He nodded, hypnotized.

She kissed him on the cheek before letting him go. "I can't take that painting," she told Jane. "I'm sorry. I thought I could, but I can't. Ford, you have it."

"I couldn't," he said.

"You must," Virginia insisted.

"I don't have a wall to hang it on."

"You'll make room," she said, misunderstanding him.

At the time he literally had no walls. He was living out of a suitcase. But she insisted. And he obliged, dragging that thing around for weeks before he settled on a property.

"I still have the painting," he told Grace, as the two finished their drinks at the bar. "It's above my mantle."

She stared, perplexed. "Is this your go-to story?"

"No," Ford said.

"I sure hope not."

"You're the only person I've told it to."

She rolled her eyes. "Is that your go-to line?"

"I'm serious," he said.

She stuck out her pinky finger. He rolled his eyes, mocking her previous gesture.

Grace clapped her hands, amused. "Are you happy?" she asked.

The question surprised Ford. As did his response.

"When I'm not thinking about it," he said.

She nodded. Her sad eyes made him happy. They made him feel less alone.

"You're easy to talk to," he told her.

"Why's that?"

"I don't know," he said. "You're just easy to talk to."

Grace joined Ford in Fitzgerald's room.

"Don't you think it's strange?" he asked, closing the door behind them. "To have told a person that?"

Grace searched the ceiling for Fitzgerald's alleged bullet hole. When she didn't find it, she used the mirror to scrutinize the room. The space was rather conventional and had long since been remodeled. Grace sat on the edge of the bed. She mentioned reading that Fitzgerald would stick his head out the room's window and shout drunken catcalls at the women below.

"But I bet that's not even the original window frame," she said.

Ford remained standing, his left shoulder to the wall. He drank too much. Grace's eyes lingered on the window. He joined her on the bed, sprawling out next to her. The ceiling spun.

"Don't you think it's strange I would have said that?" he repeated. "About my son?"

"Why'd you say it then?"

"I don't know," he said.

"Do you get out to L.A. often?" she asked.

"Not really," he said. "I mean he's usually pretty busy."

"How old is he?"

"Eighteen this December," Ford said. "I'm headed there for his birthday."

She laughed.

"I am," he said.

"Eighteen?"

"Yeah."

"How busy can an eighteen-year-old be?"

"He surfs," Ford said. "All over the world."

She considered his response. "That's wonderful," she said.

"It is wonderful," he agreed. "He's a very wonderful surfer."

His words amused them. They were both very drunk.

"But I shouldn't have said that," he said, somber once again. "To Virginia."

Grace fought back a grin before bursting with laughter.

"What's so funny?"

"You kept the painting," she said.

It took him a moment to understand. "It's a nice painting."

Grace doubled over.

Ford closed his eyes. "He can be a prick, my son."

Grace couldn't stop laughing.

Ford opened his eyes. The ceiling still spun. He closed them once more. "I shouldn't talk like that."

"He'll never know," she promised him.

"Yeah, but I will."

Grace launched into a languid rendition of "Happy Birthday." Ford eventually joined her. This too made them laugh. She leaned back on her elbows. They lay there and laughed together for a very long time. The tears stung Ford's eyes.

He awoke in the middle of the night fully dressed and dehydrated. She stood near the window with the curtain held to the side. He'd forgotten who she was and where he lay. He stumbled to the bathroom and spread out on the cold tile. She knocked, asking if he was all right. He must have said yes. He wasn't sure how long he stayed inside the bathroom, but when he stepped out she was gone.

# CHAPTER 4

Ford sipped a nightcap and studied the exchange. He'd sent the initial text—asking Grace if she'd found her wig—at 10:46 a.m. Nearly twelve hours later at 10:33 p.m. she responded: *Yes.*

He didn't know what to make of it. Or rather he knew exactly what to make of it but did not want to make it. This was her sign off. Grace's farewell. Her Dear John. It served him right. Who sends a text asking after a wig?

On his second nightcap, Ford googled JR Burnett. The third link read: "Morning sports host Jeffrey 'JR' Burnett canned after Caitlyn Jenner outburst."

He clicked the link. *The Houston Chronicle* reported:

*SportsChat, Houston's local sports radio station, announced they are parting ways with their morning host Jeffrey "JR" Burnett.*

*The announcement arrives following last week's suspension of the host, who used a homophobic and derogatory term in reference to ESPN/ABC's decision to recognize Caitlyn Jenner with the Arthur Ashe Courage Award at this year's ESPYs.*

*The suspension was handed down immediately after the show's broadcast. Shortly thereafter, Burnett offered apologies through both his Twitter and Facebook accounts, as well as an official statement through the station.*

*"I deeply regret the hurt my comments may have caused Miss Jenner as well as members of the LGBTQ community. This has been a personal and professional embarrassment. I am truly sorry."*

*Protesters gathered outside the station on Thursday, following SportsChat's announcement that they would be reinstating Burnett the following week.*

*A handful of Burnett fans gathered at the protest to support the host.*

*The opposing sides remained peaceful. By mid-afternoon the announcement arrived that SportsChat was reexamining its professional ties with Burnett.*

*On Friday morning, a smaller group of protesters gathered outside the downtown office of Ornick Oil & Gas. The company is one of Burnett's main sponsors. Its CFO, Jim Burnett, is the former radio host's father. The company pulled their sponsorship that afternoon. SportsChat announced their decision to part ways with Jeffrey Burnett shortly thereafter.*

Ford fixed a third nightcap, taking it onto his front porch. A cold evening breeze swept across the valley. He swirled the ice cube inside his glass. He knew better. There was no such thing as a second or third nightcap. This was another binge to be followed by another painful morning spent swearing off an inevitable encore.

At the bottom of the hill his neighbor's television glared. The image was too small to see, but it held Ford's attention. He didn't know much about his neighbor, which he always found strange. They were the only two homes in the immediate vicinity. Because of this he thought they would have at least exchanged names.

The neighbor approached his sliding glass door. He stood there looking out onto his property, arms akimbo. Ford had no idea what the man did for a living. No idea his age. He only knew that a woman came over every so often, but she rarely stayed the night.

Ford continued to watch his neighbor with the sense of superiority that always comes when you're the one taking notice. As if you know more than your subject simply because they're unaware they've managed your attention.

By evening's end, Ford lay on the couch listening to *The Suburbs*. Every subsequent song took a little more out of him. He'd had a good month in sales, both in the shop and online. Interest continued to grow in his prints and accessories: cell phone cases, journals, and calendars wrapped in his designs. He knew on some level this made him a hack peddling kitsch.

He also knew some of the other artists talked about him behind his back. But he'd long ago stopped caring.

"If you don't care, then why are you thinking about it?" he asked himself aloud.

"'Cause I'm drunk," he answered.

"A self-loathing drunk," he replied.

"Always," he said, and laughed before fixing a fourth drink.


He fell asleep to Arcade Fire. All night he dreamt of lost children playing capture the flag with torpedoes, hatchets, and guns. He awoke in a sweat with a chilling sense that someone was inside his house. It was three o'clock in the morning. He sat up in bed and listened. His eyes adjusted to the darkness. His bedroom door stood slightly ajar. He usually slept with it closed. He tried retracing his evening's final steps. He'd initially dozed off on the couch. He couldn't remember climbing into bed.

The house remained silent. Ford didn't own a gun or a baseball bat or a golf club. The best option he had was a set of marble bookends that Emily had given him for his twenty-fifth birthday. They were shaped as ears. He grabbed one by the lobe and approached the door. A strange calm came over him.

"Grace?" he whispered.

Silence.

"JR?"

Nothing.

He placed the giant ear onto the floor, too afraid to shut the door; afraid he'd trigger whoever or whatever awaited him on the other side. The bookend wouldn't keep the intruder out, but it would create noise if they tried entering.

Ford returned to his bed and sat on its edge, studying the black slit between the door and the frame. If a pair of eyes watched him from somewhere in that darkness they'd see only Ford's silhouette. He'd appear just as frighteningly vague to them as their invisibility was to him.

He lay down but didn't sleep. There was nothing to fear, he told himself. "Don't be an asshole," he whispered. "There's no one there."


In the morning, the giant marble ear remained where he had left it. Ford moved it aside with his foot, toppling it over. Emily's signature marked the bottom.

His glass was still on the coffee table. It contained a partially melted ice cube. Ford picked it up. A water stain marked the table. He washed the glass and placed a coaster over the new blemish.

Ford eyed Jane Fellow's encaustic painting above the mantle. He briefly imagined mailing it to Virginia Smith, wherever she might be. Wouldn't that be something? Ship the painting all these years later with a note that read: *Some of us do suffer alone.*

He laughed to reassure himself the idea was all in good fun. A sharp sting shot across is forehead. In his bathroom Ford popped two Advil, splashed cold water onto his face, and started the day.

# CHAPTER 5

Ford grew restless as the week dragged on. He knew better than to text Grace. He tried immersing himself in Bailey's collage. But *The Suburbs* remained elusive.

His other main project was far from a distraction. Grace had commissioned the piece in early October. She wanted the White Elephant track "Dear Mrs. Equitone" interpreted on the canvas. Ford was not familiar with the band, much less their album, *he do the police in different voices.* He'd spent weeks trying to decipher the lyrics. The singer relied on reverb to mask his otherwise flat vocals. The effect obscured most of his words. The internet provided little help.

Ford briefly worked on a commissioned series for a half-famous chef based out of Charlotte. The meaningless stuff always came easy. Until that is he started treating it as such. By midweek, Ford recognized the mistake, seeing his outlook reflecting back at him in mediocre work.

Tabling the chef's project, Ford shifted to miscellaneous tasks. He rearranged the gallery's layout, cleaned the fridge, organized his materials, checked inventory, put together to-do lists, and frustrated Lenny with the vacuum and bleach.

When the miscellaneous grew tedious he submitted to nostalgia, flipping through old newspaper clippings. In his early interviews Ford avoided certain aspects of his former life. Namely, surfing. At the time he wanted nothing to do with the ocean. Instead, he focused on his previous role as a business owner, shaping his narrative into that of the untapped creative stuck behind a computer screen designing business cards, flyers, van wraps, and logos.

He crafted these early accounts knowing Emily would come across the articles online. No matter how happy she and Shark Man's Facebook life appeared, Ford understood no ex could completely disavow stalking. And though he would never admit this to anyone, the early articles were all for Emily. He needed her to see him in his new life. The one she had always wanted for him. The one she imagined for them.

*Ford Carson, former business owner turned collage artist, says he never had a knack for music, outside of listening to it. At first glance inside his River Arts District studio, this passion might not be self-evident. The work itself is far from a literal interpretation of Carson's favorite songs. For example, "The River" depicts Bruce Springsteen's 1980 title track. In it a half-submerged car is used as a diving board for a pair of languid teens. The boy has a broken leg; the girl is without arms.*

*Another piece, inspired by Bob Dylan's "Tangled Up in Blues," is framed by the upper half of a head sporting a large, dark pair of sunglasses. Reflected in each lens are images plucked from the song's seven verses. The most prominent and reoccurring is a woman with various shades of red hair.*

*"If I had the talent to write these kinds of songs, maybe none of these images would exist," Carson*

*explains. "But I'm not a poet like these musicians. Words aren't something I'm good at."*

*Carson says the local music scene is what drew him to Asheville. But ultimately the mountains are what keep him around.*

*"I'm happy to be here," he says. "I always knew I'd end up here. For a while there life just kind of got in the way."*

Ford put aside the piece, devastated by its transparency. He could only imagine what Emily thought when she read it. She must have known. His intentions seemed quite obvious.

"I could live here," he remembered Emily telling him.

The two stared at the distant mountains.

They had visited Asheville in the summer of 2005. Their final trip as a couple. They spent it pretending. Pretending that the trip itself was just a trip, not a last-ditch effort to save their marriage. Pretending that Emily's mother had volunteered to watch Bailey out of goodwill as opposed to sheer desperation for her daughter's family. Pretending that the room on the fifth floor of the Grove Park Inn was all they needed. Pretending that their evening drinks out on the terrace would be enough to keep them pretending the next day and the day after that and the day after that.

"I could live here," she repeated.

Ford contemplated his old fashioned. Emily sipped her chilled white wine.

"Is that smoke?" he asked, pointing toward the golf course.

"Steam," Emily said. "The bartender told me the hut out there is where the hotel cleans all its towels and linens."

"That's a lot of steam."

"They've got a lot of towels and linens."

They both sipped their drinks and looked out at the mountains.

"It's beautiful out here," she said.

Ford nodded.

"I could live here," she repeated for a third time.

"It'd be a nice place to retire," Ford agreed.

"No, I mean now."

Ford remained silent. Emily finished her wine.

"Jesus, that really is a lot of steam," Ford said.

"We've never left Dania," she continued, refusing to back down.

"Why do you always discredit Gainesville?"

"Because college doesn't count," she said. "I didn't even graduate."

Ford refused to look at her. Here they were on a trip to get away and all she could talk about was how they never got away. He finished his old fashioned.

"It feels different here," she said. "There's history to this place. We don't have that in Dania."

"There's history in Dania," Ford said, feeling better from the drink. "We got jai alai."

She laughed a single harsh note and shook her head. "There's a history of convenience in Dania, but that's about it."

Ford eyed his empty glass, watching the ice cube slowly melt. "Why can't you just enjoy things?"

"Do you know that every time you tell me to *enjoy things*, all I hear is *ignore*?"

"Actually, I do," Ford said. "Because you've used that line on me about a thousand times."

"My point exactly," she said.

"You know you're unbelievable," he told her. "All these mountains. The wine. The meals. And this is what it gets me?"

Emily sat silent, her eyes straight ahead, staring out toward the rising steam.


They had been each other's first and like all firsts they shouldn't have extended beyond high school. But they had. Even after Emily moved five hours north to study English in Gainesville. They initially took turns visiting each other until Emily's workload impeded her travels. Ford tried convincing her to get the books on tape to listen to on her drive down the turnpike.

"I'm not up here reading John Grisham novels," she informed him.

"I didn't say you were."

"You don't respect what I do."

"Yes I do," Ford said.

"You do what?"

"I respect what you do. I couldn't do it."

"What couldn't you do?"

"Read all those books."

They briefly split up that spring. Ford drank a lot and thought about dating but held out hope that they would get back together. That what they needed was just what she'd claimed: space.

Emily had other plans. Ford had met his replacement (a pretentious little bastard with a real hard-on for the word *kitsch*) at a party prior to their split. At the time Ford didn't know what *kitsch* meant. Emily did, or at least she laughed each time Kitsch Boy said it. Eventually, Ford laughed too. This, no doubt, had been Kitsch Boy's plan all along.

"What's so funny?" Kitsch Boy asked.

It was late. The party was dying down.

"What you said," Ford answered.

"Why's it funny?" Kitsch Boy insisted.

"Because it's true."

"What's true?"

"It's very kitsch," Ford said.

"What's kitsch?"

"Everything on that table."

"No," Kitsch Boy said. "I mean literally. What does *kitsch* mean?"

Ford thumbed the lip of his beer bottle.

"You don't know what it means."

"It means go fuck yourself," Ford said.

"Jesus, Ford," Emily whispered.

Kitsch Boy laughed, before wishing Emily a good evening. That's how he said it too. *Good evening.* He then looked at Ford and shook his head, offering a contemptuous huff.

Ford charged him. He could still see the transformation from the smug to the terrified. Kitsch Boy had been raised on a promise that if you kept a certain class of friends you could patronize and critique to your heart's content without the slightest fear of a true human response. That had always been Ford's issue with Emily's college friends. They could theorize every aspect of life. They could deconstruct and reference the esoteric. But they didn't know shit.

Emily was horrified. She thought Ford had smashed his beer bottle over Kitsch Boy's head. In reality, Kitsch Boy had nicked his forehead on the doorknob as he fell back. And if there's one thing a head's good for it's bleeding. So it bled and Emily yelled and another partygoer helped Kitsch Boy up and Emily took him to the hospital.

Ford stayed behind. The party's host insisted that he leave, but Ford had nowhere to go. He ended up sleeping on the couch. At five in the morning, Emily woke him. By then he'd forgotten about the entire fracas. Forgot he was sleeping on a stranger's couch. He asked Emily what they were doing. She told him he ought to go home.

Of course, Kitsch Boy didn't last. The summer arrived and Emily returned to Dania. She and Ford reconciled. It was the summer of '96, but it felt like they'd time traveled back to their first meeting on the beach. Only they managed to stretch that feeling the entire twelve weeks. They talked about marriage and kids and the places they would go and the things they'd see and all the other stuff you say during the summer when nothing is quite as real as the fall, winter, and spring.

When Emily returned to Gainesville, so too did her impatience and dissatisfaction. This time around, though, her focus broadened. It didn't apply exclusively to Ford but to everyone. Particularly herself. Nevertheless, they managed to make it to winter, then spring.

"Do you realize how easy we have it?" she asked Ford.

This became Emily's mantra throughout her sophomore year. Back then she held a general contempt for all of life's advantages. An insistence on a world unbalanced, a world corrupt, a world completely fucked.

But over time the veneer cracked. Her outrage had little to do with the system and everything to do with herself. Emily was experiencing an existential crisis. She had decided to become a writer. But what exactly did she have to write about? What insights could the daughter of a litigator offer the world? Where did six years of horse camp fall into the sort of narrative she'd dreamt necessary to truly claim a voice? What inspiration did she have to draw from? What struggles had she faced?

She never voiced her concerns outright. If anything, she projected her fears onto Ford. "Don't you get scared?" she asked. "You literally don't know anything outside of Dania. And all that you do know has already happened. You'll be following in your dad's footsteps even though you already know how that story goes."

"It's a family business."

"Only if you continue it," she said.

"It makes sense to."

"If you're looking for the easy way out."

"It'll benefit us both," he said.

Emily fell silent.

He knew then he was losing her again. Only this time it felt less personal. He sensed her loss. She didn't want to lose him, but it was beyond her control.

This was the final day of spring break. And they both knew it was goodbye. And so they drank a proper farewell. And stumbled to the beach. And fucked under the pier. And listened to the waves. And said silly things. And laughed. And cried. And took turns saying pretty things to help the other one stop crying.

It all felt right. Ford remembered being okay with it then. Knowing that it was the end but that they would see each other again in different lives and under different circumstances. That the transition would be the hardest part. But once they got through that, all would be fine.

Emily returned in May. They hadn't spoken since their farewell night. She found him inside his father's print shop. He stood behind the counter entering payments. She remained by the door, peering out its front window onto A-1A. Her face reflected off the glass. At first her focus stayed on the traffic. Then she looked toward his reflection in the window. They stared at each through the glass. Neither moved. She must have been deciding things. The door stood two feet away. Ford still didn't know what gesture he made, but whatever he'd done caused her to smile. It wasn't a broad smile by any means. If anything it was more in her eyes than her lips. And maybe it had nothing to do with Ford. Maybe it was the fact that she'd accepted the situation. Maybe it was the smile of surrender.

"I'm pregnant," Emily told him.

Ford found his most recent profile in *NatGeo*. He glanced over a short passage. The selection was enough to make one thing clear: If the early write-ups were to impress Emily, the later stuff all carried the hope of reaching his son.

> *"It's a challenge," Carson explains. "I used to surf in another life. And so I tend to think of collage a lot like I thought of riding waves. At best the ocean doesn't care; at worst it doesn't want you there. You've got to find a way to earn your place. That's like collage. You've got all these disparate images that don't belong together. Maybe they don't even want to be together. My job is to figure it out and make them fit."*

His ex-wife and Shark Man left Dania two years after they wed, relocating with Bailey to Cocoa Beach.

"It only makes sense," Emily told Ford several months before the move. "We're spending practically every weekend up there for the waves."

"We got waves down here too," Ford said.

"I don't think you realize how committed your son is."

"You're moving to Cocoa Beach," Ford said. "I think I realize."

"Have you considered?" she asked.

"I'm not selling the business."

"Then I guess that settles things," she said. "We'll meet halfway every other weekend."

For a period the distance improved Ford's relationship with his son. In Bailey's absence the ocean took on a deeper meaning. It became a giant blanket that held them together, stretching the entire one hundred and eighty-eight miles between Dania and Cocoa Beach.

Ford committed to surfing every day. Along with riding the waves, he sought out documentaries, films, magazines, and books on the sport. His efforts briefly paid off. Bailey not only seemed to listen to Ford's ideas, he also appeared to actually consider and enjoy what his father had to say.

"If you pay attention it'll show you things," Ford promised his son. "What we're doing is way more than a sport. I mean think about it. In totality we're actually riding waves for less than ten percent of the time. And when we do catch one it's what? seven, eight seconds? But we don't think of it that way do we? Why would we?"

By thirteen, Bailey's interest in his father's meditations came to an abrupt and critical end. "Nobody gives a fuck," he shouted during a weekend visit to Dania.

The exclamation startled Ford. Not so much the words but his son's tone. He didn't recognize Bailey's voice. And though he knew this day would come, he never actually expected it to arrive.

"And if you surfed them more than you talked them maybe I wouldn't have to catch so much shit from everybody about my weirdo dad," Bailey continued.

Ford's throat clenched. "I didn't realize your friends think I'm weird."

"Well you are," Bailey assured him, grabbing his board and heading for the water.

That afternoon they took the turnpike north to Port St. Lucy, the halfway point between Dania and Cocoa Beach. Neither spoke the entire ride.

"Mom wants to talk to you," Bailey finally said, as Ford pulled into a parking space at the rest stop.

"About what?" Ford asked, looking over at this son.

Bailey shook his head, staring down at his hands. "She just wants to talk to you," he said.

Ford was incensed. An hour and a half drive and Bailey couldn't have given him a prior heads-up.

Emily approached the car, opening the passenger side door. Bailey immediately asked if he should go get ice cream. Ford would remember the question later on. Because his son hadn't asked *for* ice cream; he had specifically asked his mother *if* he should go get ice cream. Like it was punishment. Emily hurried him the money. Ford instinctively called after him, fearful to be alone with his ex-wife. But Bailey was gone. Ford faced Emily. The wind blew her dirty blonde hair to the side, briefly concealing her right eye.

"I'm pregnant," she said.

He could no longer look at her. Even though he knew by not looking at her he revealed just as much, if not more. He hadn't expected the news to hit him the way it had. He hadn't expected the news at all. The tips of his fingers tingled.

He finally had the sense to offer his congratulations. Emily's arms uncrossed, hanging listlessly at her sides. For a brief moment it looked as if she might reach for him. Of course, she didn't. They stood there awkwardly before they both nodded, uncertain. She then confessed that she'd been nervous all weekend about how he'd handle the news. With that they said their goodbyes.

Ford drove back to Dania in silence. The yellow remains of dragonflies gathered on his windshield. The sky was dark by the time he took his exit. He remembered thinking it before half-wishing he'd said it. But the opportunity had long since passed. So instead he screamed the words inside his car: "I thought you didn't want more kids!"

# CHAPTER 6

Grace leaned against his car, smiling as Ford approached. Her hands pressed deep inside her coat pockets. He hadn't expected to find her outside his studio. Her gray eyes narrowed with playful suspicion as he neared. Ford paused, holding up his hands in equally playful surrender.

She laughed, and he continued toward her. They kissed as if it was a given. And they continued to kiss as if a week hadn't passed without a single word between them. But he didn't mind.

"Take a ride with me," she said, leading him to her car. It was neither a question nor a command. Not even a statement really. Just a fact. An inevitable fact.

"Where we headed?" he asked.

"It's a surprise," she said.

Despite their reunion's initial ease, silence marked several miles of their drive. It didn't bother Ford, though. He was happy to be with her.

"How have you been?" he asked.

Her head swayed rhythmically, despite the radio's silence. "Good," she said, ending the conversation.

The sun gradually set behind the mountains as they crossed into Tennessee. Ford tried again. "Should I have packed a toothbrush?" he joked.

"What's the matter?" Grace asked, eyes on the road. "You don't like surprises?"

Her tone was unsettling. Ford changed the subject. He told her about Bailey's new birthday plans. How his son was set to come east rather than Ford going west. She called the news exciting, though she didn't sound excited.

"He'll be eighteen," Ford said, just to say it.

She turned on the radio. The jingle to Al's Pawnshop played. *If you got old junk that you want to swap / If you're in a funk, come to Al's Pawnshop.*

Grace changed the station without comment.


Bright bulbs outlined the Funland sign, a small amusement park just east of Gatlinburg. Ford followed Grace through the outdoor crowd, passing bumper cars and a rundown go-kart track. They ended up at Thunder Road, a wooden roller coaster with a handwritten note at its gate announcing that it was the final weekend to ride before it shut down for the season. Its farewell tour drew an unimpressive crowd.

They sat in the front car. The attendant, a teenage boy, locked them in. Once the bar was set, the young employee looked at Grace. His dull, tired eyes widened.

"You're that girl," he said.

She ignored him.

The ride slowly climbed out of the gate.

"Billy," the attendant called back to one of his pals. "It's her!"

82

At the top of the track, before the drop, Grace clutched Ford's knee and said something, but the wind pulled her words out of reach. The car jerked to the left, then dropped, circling back around before climbing a slope. Behind them a small boy screamed that he wanted off.

Grace leaned into Ford. He anticipated her tongue's wet kiss inside his ear. Instead, she shouted, "I'm so fucking depressed."

By then the boy was crying behind them. Ford tried turning to see him, but the ride shot through a brief tunnel before taking a shallow dip.

"Make it stop," the boy screamed.

As if answering the boy's plea, the ride came to a halt. They pulled up to the loading station. Only a few people waited in line. Grace let go of Ford's knee.

"You ain't gonna ride it again?" the attendant asked.

Once more Grace ignored the teenage boy, leaving the platform. The attendant and his pal Billy both stood silent, watching her walk toward the arcade.

Ford considered the boys. "You know her?" he asked them.

The two eyed Ford. "No sir," the attendant finally spoke, kicking at the ground. "She just comes here a bunch. Always riding the coaster."

Ford left the pair, passing a bench where the fearful little boy clung to his father's neck, sobbing.

The cherry red pleather reflected the ceiling's florescent and neon lights. Children ran from Skee-Ball to virtual racecars to basketball hoops. Ford sat across from Grace. Her eyes held his with deep suspicion.

"What did Bethany tell you?" she asked.

He leaned into the table. A dried soda spill stuck to his forearm. He pulled away, rubbing off the sugar.

"I'm just curious," Grace said, her eyes suddenly soft and reassuring. "She claims she can't remember."

"She was pretty stoned," Ford said, backing Bethany's claim.

"Yeah, but what'd she say?"

"She talked a lot about her husband sleeping with the nanny," Ford said.

Grace rolled her eyes.

"She did."

"I don't doubt it," Grace said.

A small boy approached them, placing a sleeve of tickets on the table before realizing that Ford and Grace were not his parents. The boy retrieved the tickets in a quiet hurry and ran off.

"What else did she tell you?" Grace asked, as if the boy had never been there.

Ford considered the question. He thought about telling her the truth. But most of what Bethany had told him was rumor.

"What do you want me to say?" he asked.

Grace retrieved a sugar packet from the table and rubbed it between her fingers. "I want you to say what you think."

"I think people are complicated," he said.

Grace cocked her head, unimpressed. Ford ran his tongue over his back right molar and waited.

"Well, none of it's true," she said.

A slight tear in the packet released a slow stream of sugar gathering like sand at the bottom of an hourglass. Grace placed the packet on its side.

"What's the biggest lie you've ever told?" she asked.

"I don't know," Ford said, after some consideration. "I guess I always focused on managing the smaller ones."

"Don't be funny."

"I'm not trying to make you laugh."

"I don't know what to do," she said.

"Why are we here?" he asked.

"Tonight was the last chance to ride Thunder Road."

"And we rode it."

She focused on the sugar packet. "I was always the one with the secrets," she said. "Not Jeffrey. That's what I liked about him. He seemed wonderfully uncomplicated. Almost absurdly so."

She continued to stare at the packet before returning her attention to Ford. "But that's the thing about secrets," she said. "When you keep them long enough, you start thinking you're the only one who's got them."

Dr. Hudson's students practically lived at the Hudson home. Grace couldn't remember a family dinner without at least one or two of the professor's pupils attending, she told Ford. Some made weekly appearances. Others came and went. ("A dubious scab laying down the groundwork for a future recommendation for some future law school application for some future-future they can't stop planning out," her father would lament.)

His students at the small liberal arts college in Yellow Springs, Ohio regarded Dr. Hudson as the patron saint of the Beatnik culture. His command as English professor, however, did not translate in most other facets of his life. He struggled greatly as a father. He didn't know how to relate to children. Whenever Grace approached him to share a story, or to try out a joke, or to show off a high test score, Dr. Hudson would listen impatiently, scratching at the sides of his head while biting down on his bottom lip, nodding compulsively as if the gesture might wrap things up a bit quicker. Once she completed her story/joke/update, Dr. Hudson would remain still, staring at her with a bewildered brow, fearful to move as if it might trigger additional anecdotes.

"So then that concludes things?" he would say.

And Grace would nod.

And Dr. Hudson would mirror her response.

"I've got a lot to do, Gray," he'd tell her. "These books don't read themselves."

At twelve, Grace discovered that Beat poetry was the way to her father's heart. She spent hours each day inside her room memorizing entire poems, which Dr. Hudson had her recite each night before their dinner guests. Throughout these performances the professor would nod gratuitously, swirling the last of his wine. Meanwhile, Grace's mother Nancy simply watched, often from the kitchen away from the crowd.

A year in, Grace overheard a pair of her father's students speculating about her age. When Dr. Hudson summoned her that evening to deliver poems from Diane di Prima's *This Kind of Bird Flies Backward*, Grace refused.

After his guests departed, Dr. Hudson berated Grace. "What the hell was that?" he demanded. "You embarrassed yourself tonight. You absolutely embarrassed yourself. Jesus Christ, Grace! Those are my colleagues."

"Your colleagues?" Nancy erupted, coming to her daughter's defense. "Directionless and impressionable freshmen are now your colleagues? Give me a fucking break, Gary."

Dr. Hudson laughed and applauded Nancy's insults, accusing her of jealousy, insisting that she resented seeing in his colleagues what she herself once possessed: passion.

"You are a delusional, pathetic, and desperate fraud," Nancy said, leaving the room.

In the coming days when Nancy wasn't around, Dr. Hudson begged. "Gray, you have to," he pleaded. "You're the talk of the town. And listen. Are you listening, goddamn it? Who do I have besides you, huh? Your mother? Nobody wants to listen to your mother. Your mother bathes dogs for a living. She performs anal expressions. These aren't topics people want to hear while they're eating. They want to hear you."

But Grace refused.

Without her, dinner and wine soon turned into beer and cigarettes on the front porch. Laughter filled the late evenings as undergraduates stumbled into the home, looking for the bathroom. Eventually, beer and cigarettes turned into whiskey and weed.

Her parents argued. Dr. Hudson spent days away from the house, returning only to shower or do laundry. Grace resented him. But even then she knew it reactionary, a defense against hurt.

When she later discovered that hurt outlasted bitterness, Grace rejoined her father and his newest batch of adoring pupils on the front porch. Dr. Hudson neither invited nor denied her entry into the circle. Perhaps he didn't recognize her, mistaking his thirteen-year-old daughter for just another disciple. One of the boys offered her a cigarette. Grace accepted, waiting for her father to object. He never did.

All the while, Nancy slept inside. Every night, she went to bed a little earlier than the last. And so every night, Grace's evenings unfolded in a similar pattern: a cigarette, a sip of whiskey, a glass of whiskey, some weed.

By fourteen, Grace was involved with a number of her father's students, desperate to leave her scent on all their tongues so that Dr. Hudson would have to smell her in every lecture hall. She'd bring home these boys during the daytime hours. Periods when she knew her mother was at work but when her father might not be. Whenever she heard his keys hit the counter, Grace would fuck a little louder despite her bedroom door being wide open. She wanted to force Dr. Hudson to look inside. To see.

And one day he did. Father and daughter held brief eye contact. Then Dr. Hudson continued down the hall.

"If your intention is to sleep with my entire roster," he told her later that day, "could you, at the very least, do so behind closed doors?"

There were eight total. None lovers. Just bodies she hoped might snap the professor.

By fifteen, Grace grew more selective. She'd observe Dr. Hudson's interactions on the front porch. Who did he look to for discussion? Who showed up again and again? Who did he glance toward while in conversation with others?

That's how Grace settled on Chelsea. The two kissed after sharing a cigarette on the side of the Hudson home. The brief exchange ended with Chelsea laughing and lighting another smoke and talking about one of the boys at the gathering—how she couldn't stand how pompous and ostentatious and brazen he was.

Grace asked which boy. Chelsea shook her head, muttering that Grace didn't know him. Grace knew everyone. Chelsea continued eyeing the earth, babbling. That's how Grace knew Chelsea was fucking Dr. Hudson. She wanted to slap the stupid girl. Instead, she kissed Chelsea again, pressing her tongue against Chelsea's locked teeth until the bones parted. Chelsea bit down in protest, pinching Grace's muscle until it bled.

"I'm not a dyke," Chelsea said, turning the corner to rejoin the party.

Grace remained in the shadows. The blood eased down her throat. It tasted like copper.

Within days, Chelsea returned to the house to see Grace. The two sat on the porch. Cigarette butts and empty bottles littered the floor, coated in a layer of yellow pollen. Chelsea wore a shawl despite the late spring heat.

Grace pulled out a pack of cigarettes.

Chelsea declined. "I only smoke when I'm drunk."

Grace shrugged, lighting up.

"How old are you anyway?" Chelsea asked.

"That's a very conventional approach to conversation," Grace said, blowing smoke in Chelsea's direction.

Chelsea fanned the air. "You sound like Gary."

"He is my father," she said, hating Chelsea for calling him by his first name.

"Neither of you are as smart as you think you are."

"I'm just a needy slut," Grace said, repeating past accusations made against her by several sad, angry boys.

"That's what I don't get about you," Chelsea said. "I mean you've slept with like everyone in my class."

"I'm a needy slut," Grace repeated.

"Guys!" Chelsea said. "You slept with guys!"

Grace nodded.

"So then why'd you do that the other night?" Chelsea asked, looking toward the side of the property as if she needed to remind Grace of their kiss. "I mean if you're so into guys?"

"You looked pretty, I guess."

"I don't look pretty now?"

"You're wearing too much makeup," Grace said. "You're trying too hard."

"What the hell are you?"

"Just a needy slut."

Chelsea stood, hovering over Grace. "You and your father have the same eyes."

Grace tried to kiss her just to shut her up. Chelsea pulled away, scanning the street and neighboring homes. Grace stepped inside, leaving the door open.

"Where are you going?" Chelsea called after her.

Grace continued up the stairs, certain that Chelsea would follow, though she wasn't entirely sure she wanted her to. The two kissed on her bed. Grace kept her eyes open as Chelsea blindly undressed her. Within minutes, Grace wore only socks. Meanwhile, Chelsea remained clothed, kissing her way down Grace's body.

Grace stared at the ceiling and imagined she was a man. Imagined her erection inside Chelsea's mouth. She pulled off Chelsea's shawl and grabbed a hold of her brown hair, wrapping it around her right fist and tugging on it the same way some of the sad, angry boys had tugged on her hair.

"You're hurting me," Chelsea cried.

Grace released her. Chelsea ran her hands over her scalp, making sure none of her hair had been torn out. Once satisfied, Chelsea removed her own shirt and then continued going down on Grace. Within a few minutes, Chelsea did for Grace what none of the others could.

Despite its initial euphoria, the orgasm disturbed Grace. She didn't know what it meant or why it happened. She hurried on her underwear.

"What are you doing?" Chelsea teased.

Grace continued to dress.

"What are you doing?" Chelsea repeated.

Grace put on her shirt.

"What the fuck are you doing?" Chelsea demanded.

"Getting dressed."

"Why?"

"I'm finished," she said.

"What about me?"

"I don't want to," Grace said.

"What do you mean you don't want to?"

"I don't want to," Grace repeated.

"But you have to," Chelsea said.

"No, I don't."

Chelsea pulled Grace toward the bed. "I went down on you."

"Fuck off."

The two words made her feel powerful. How many times had the sad, angry boys directed the exact same phrase at her?

Chelsea threw Grace aside, hurrying on her shirt and shawl. "You dumb, stupid dyke," she shouted.

Grace just stood there.

"You *are* a nasty, little slut," Chelsea continued.

The accusation did not affect Grace. Not in the way Chelsea had intended. It hurt Grace, but only because it made her empathize with Chelsea. Like an out-of-body experience, she suddenly saw her own helplessness through this half-naked girl.

Grace stepped toward Chelsea and embraced her. The gesture calmed Chelsea. The two hugged. Grace felt on the verge of tears until Chelsea's hands made their way down her back. Grace was still only in her underwear and shirt. Chelsea's hands were now massaging her. Grace stepped away.

"Come here," Chelsea whispered.

"That's not what I meant."

Chelsea huffed. "Jesus Christ, you really are like Gary."

Grace slapped Chelsea and threw her to the ground.

"Just like Gary," Chelsea repeated.

Grace scratched violently at her face. Chelsea screamed and tried to fight back, but Grace held down Chelsea's arms with her knees. All the while, she continued into Chelsea, punching and slapping and scratching and spitting. But after the initial shock of the violence wore off, Grace's abuse seemed only to invigorate Chelsea, who repeated the fact that Grace was *just like Gary, just like Gary, just like Gary.*

The front door opened. Grace was deaf to its noise and deaf to the subsequent footsteps on the stairs.

"What are you doing? What are you doing?" her mother screamed, pulling Grace off Chelsea.

Chelsea crawled toward the bedroom door, gasping for air. Nancy tried helping her. Chelsea shrieked. "Don't touch me," she cried out. "Don't *fucking* touch me."

"But are you okay?" Nancy asked.

Chelsea glared at Nancy until her lungs calmed. "Your husband and daughter," she finally said, eyeing Grace briefly before smiling at Nancy. "I've fucked them both."

The Thunder Road attendant sat on the trunk of an old Toyota Corolla, smoking a cigarette. When Ford and Grace passed by the teenage boy, he quickly discarded the smoke.

"Thought I saw me a shooting star," he called out nervously.

The boy's presence startled Grace. He apologized, holding up both hands. Grace continued to press down on her chest, exhaling deeply. The boy looked at Ford briefly for guidance. Ford offered none.

The boy pointed up at the sky, repeating the fact that he saw a shooting star.

"Well, did you make a wish?" Grace asked.

"No, ma'am," the boy said, rubbing his neck. "Turned out it was a plane."

"A plane?" she asked. "Was it crashing?"

"I sure don't think so!" the boy exclaimed, looking back up at the sky. "Hope not anyway."

"What I mean is how do you mistake the two?"

The boy again glanced at Ford for guidance. Once more Ford offered none.

"Might have been a shooting star," the boy said. "I don't know. Pretty sure she was a plane, though."

"You should make a wish all the same," Grace said.

"Okay," the boy answered, looking to get away. "Maybe I will."

"Would you like me to tell you what to wish for?" she asked, stepping closer.

The boy crossed his arms. "I suppose I could wish you a good evening."

Grace laughed. "You aren't as stupid as you look," she told him.

Her words shocked Ford.

"And you aren't as pretty as you think," the boy answered.

"I meant that as a compliment," Grace said.

"I sure as hell didn't."

"Well, aren't you something tough," she mocked him.

The boy looked at Ford. "I can get mean, mister."

Grace laughed, throwing herself into Ford's arms. "Oh darling—save me, save me!"

Ford led her to the car.

"Save me," she continued to cry out, laughing.

"Fuck you," the boy called after them.

Ford hurried her along. "What's wrong with you?" he asked, once they reached the car.

She pressed into him, resting her cheek against his chest. "Like it never happens to you," she said, looking up at him. "Doesn't it?"

Ford opened the passenger side door and helped her in. She didn't contest. The entire drive home she rested her head on his shoulder, staring out into the darkness.


They ended the night at his place. He made them drinks. When they finished, she asked if he was having another. He served them both a second round.

"That was very cruel, what I said to that boy."

"It was a little mean," Ford agreed.

"How do you do it?" she asked. "How do you always stay so calm?"

"I don't."

"I've never seen you snap," she said. "Not once."

"Give it time."

"You don't have it in you."

He didn't know what to say. She had no basis for her claim. But he didn't mind the man she perceived him to be. Maybe that was how you became someone else.

She continued admiring him, her head tilted to the side, studying his silence like it spoke volumes. "I really don't think you do," she said.

He shrugged.

She stood, leaning over the counter to kiss him, tugging at his shirt as if the gesture alone would pull him across the surface. He stepped around the counter. She took his hand, leading him to the bedroom as if she owned the place.

# CHAPTER 7

The subject line stated: SHELLFISH ALLERGY. Emily's actual email read:

> *I've attached a file with a list of food items Bailey CANNOT eat. He'll try and tell you otherwise. It's mostly shellfish: shrimp, crab, lobster, oysters. His eyes swelled shut for three days the last time. Please print this out before he arrives. That way you don't have to play the bad guy. You can just show him the list and tell him I told him no. His doctor says he's lucky his esophagus didn't close.*
>
> *I'm not trying to be overwhelming. He's just stubborn. If I didn't stop him, he'd kill himself on seafood. Between that and his surfing, he's still very much your son.*
>
> *I know he hasn't been very communicative about the visit, but he's very excited*
>
> *—Emily*

The coffee percolated. Ford tried remembering the end of the night. He wasn't sure when Grace left or how she managed to drive home.

Sipping his coffee, he read back over Emily's email. Her implications annoyed him. He started, stopped, and subsequently erased several responses before he needed a refill.

Only then did he see Grace's note. She'd written it on the back of a receipt and left it next to the whiskey bottle.

*Ford,*
*I'm leaving you and taking the kids ;)*
*xoxo*
*Grace*

He read it over twice more. *Don't overthink it,* he told himself. He forced a laugh, which hurt his head. Ford placed the note back on the countertop and left the kitchen, forgetting to refill his mug.

Nauseated, he stretched across the couch and stared at Jane Fellow's painting. A giant colorful wave that never quite crashed.

After reading back over Emily's email, he attempted one more response.

*Thanks Emily. Sure glad to know the Carson self-destructive gene lives on. Nothing a father loves to hear more. But if that's truly the case, I fear our reunion will be disastrous. Thank goodness for your printout. Always the responsible one, you are. It must be exhausting.*

Ford canceled the message, throwing his phone across the room.

"Fucking bitch," he muttered.

Throughout their marriage he drank. Initially, Emily made light of it. She'd give him nicknames like Cowboy and say things like, "Slow down, Cowboy." But on nights when Cowboy didn't slow down, she'd ditch the pet name and remind him of a pending work deadline, or insist he was going to wake Bailey, or lambast him over the fact that it was a fucking Tuesday night.

"Is this really how you want to spend the rest of your life?" she once asked.

"It's how I relax."

"No, it's how you mask," she said.

"How I *mask?*"

"Your work. Our marriage. Everything," she said. "You aren't happy. I'm not happy. And we'll never be happy. Not here. And not if you keep this up."

Near the end of their marriage, she began lining his previous evening's bottles in front of the coffeemaker, requiring Ford to move them aside each morning to brew a pot. He ignored the signal, treating it instead as an inconvenience, mumbling that if she hated the mess so much why not just take the extra step and throw them away herself.

His drinking worsened once they split. And worsened still, once Emily and Bailey moved to Cocoa Beach. He didn't hit rock bottom, though, until Emily invited him to speak at Bailey's eighth grade career day.

Ford arrived at the middle school tipsy. He checked his eyes in the rearview mirror as he folded a piece of gum into his mouth. Across the parking lot, he spotted Shark Man's Volvo with its goddamn New Day Rising bumper sticker. The thought of Shark Man in the audience infuriated Ford. He considered leaving. Instead, he took another swig, infusing whiskey into his stick of peppermint gum.

"You must be Mr. Carson," a woman's voice called as he entered the classroom.

Ford didn't respond. He focused on Emily, who sat alone in the back row. The swig had improved his outlook. He was ready to stare Shark Man down. But now there was no Shark Man. Just his ex-wife. And she refused to acknowledge him.

"Mr. Carson," the same voice called out. "Please join us."

He turned toward the speaker. The teacher smiled and waved him forward. Shark Man was seated among the presenters. He nodded quietly in Ford's direction. Ford spit his gum into the trash bin and proceeded to the front.

Shark Man played opener. He spent the first five minutes discussing his law practice and the second five minutes promoting his band. He must have said *New Day Rising* fifteen times within that brief window. Near the end of his talk, he surprised the class with burned copies of the group's latest home recording.

Ford watched in horror as Bailey smiled, nodding at a classmate knowingly. Did his son actually like New Day

Rising? Did he think Shark Man was anything more than just a sad, middle-aged wannabe Bono?

"Fucking bullshit," Ford muttered.

"What's wrong with you?" a fellow presenter chided him.

Ford turned to the offended woman. She wore a white lab coat. "It's ridiculous," he insisted. "This is career day. Why should we have to suffer through this guy's pipe dream?"

"That's somebody's father," the woman said in a sharp whisper.

"No," Ford said. "That's the best part—he's not."

The woman turned away from Ford, ending the conversation.

After the music was distributed, Shark Man held up one of the CDs and waved it in the air. "This," he said, "is important. And I say it not because it's my music. The reason I offer you this is because I think it's crucial to remind children that you aren't defined by your profession. I'm not merely Timothy Warwick, the lawyer. I'm also Timothy Warwick, the musician, the gardener, the grill master, the husband, the father, and maybe even the guy who can't say no to chocolate."

The class laughed like a well-trained studio audience. Even Bailey got in on it. Shark Man ate it up, smiling and looking out onto the crowd.

"But in all seriousness," he continued, still holding the CD above his head. "Even if you don't like my songs, keep that message in mind. Because it's your passions and how you share these passions that count the most. That's my spiel. Thank you and rock on."

The class applauded. Ford glared at Emily. Had this been her ploy the whole time? To force Ford to drive three hours north to listen to her husband's beaming outlook. The clapping continued as Shark Man made his way to the back of the room. Emily gleamed with pride. When the teacher called Ford's name, he didn't respond. He couldn't look away from Emily and Shark Man. The two spoke and nodded and waved to Bailey before exiting the classroom together.

"You're up," the woman in the white lab coat said, shooing Ford away.

It took a handful of guided questions to get Ford going. Even then it was a distracted talk.

"Well, Mr. Carson, maybe you could tell us the hardest part about owning a business," the teacher suggested.

Emily stepped back into the classroom. Ford's pulse quickened. He waited for Shark Man to follow, but Emily closed the door gently behind her.

"The hardest part of owning a business?" he repeated the question aloud for Emily's benefit.

The teacher nodded.

Emily sat down. For a brief moment they made eye contact. She offered something like a smile. Perhaps taking pity on what must have appeared an unqualified speaker. Within that split second, Ford imagined a bizarre universe where they were still married. And while certainly not a perfect marriage (not even in the bizarre version), she'd come to watch and support him on career day.

"There's a lot of sacrifice," Ford said.

Bailey dragged an eraser back and forth across the surface of his desk. He hadn't been that way when Shark Man spoke. He'd listened.

"You have to sacrifice," Ford repeated, practically shouting the words at his son.

Bailey continued to grind away his eraser.

"I, of course, inherited the business," Ford continued. "It was my father's. And that's something that's often misunderstood. People assume inheritance is the equivalent of a gift. And now I'm not going to stand here and deny that all together. Certainly you've got a leg up when you inherit a business. But there are downsides. Just like with everything in life. The truth is, nothing comes easy. That's something I think is worth noting. When you're young, people try and sell you certain narratives. Do this, that, and the other and everything else will fall into place. But that's never the case. There is no place. No equation for life."

He paused, frustrated with Bailey, who had yet to acknowledge his presence. "See, I surf. A lot like my son," Ford said, pointing at his boy.

The class turned their heads in unison to study Bailey. At first Ford thought they didn't know Bailey surfed. A short-lived theory. Behind Emily, hung a framed newspaper article about Bailey's recent first place finish. Ford stared at the article while the class continued to stare at his son. Ford understood then that they looked toward Bailey out of confusion. They hadn't realized Ford was his father.

"My name is Ford *Carson*," he shouted. "Bailey Carson is my son."

"Well, thank you, Mr. Carson," the teacher said.

"I'm not finished," Ford insisted.

All the kids' heads snapped forward. Even Bailey briefly looked up. Emily stared Ford down. He stared her back before continuing.

"It's like I tell my son when we're out there on the water. Life *is* the ocean. I mean you're talking this massive body of water with waves coming at you. And these waves you're seeing—that's only the half of it. Underneath the surface is an equally strong current thrashing you about. And beneath that and farther out there's an entire history of shipwrecks and sharks and oil spills and lost treasures. You're swimming among the living and the dead and the deadly. And that's the thing with a business. There are so many unseen variables. It requires—"

Emily stood, making her way toward the door. Only then did Ford notice her slight bump. Everything slowed as he stared at her profile. Was this why she'd invited him? Had this been the plan all along? Or had she not even thought to tell him? Had he become that much of an afterthought?

The subsequent realization nearly broke him: he was now officially outnumbered. Shark Man would have two kids to his one. And Ford's one was more like a half. He looked at Bailey, who had returned to dragging his eraser across the surface of his desk. Shark Man was making Ford irrelevant.

"My best advice," Ford said, quickening his words to reach Emily before her departure, "would be to not have children. If you really want to make a go at what you want to do, don't get yourself locked in. Who knows what we could have been? Maybe I could have been something good. Hell, you could have been a writer."

Emily turned around, throwing her hands up in disbelief. *Why?* she mouthed, *why?*

"Not that kids are a bad thing," Ford said. "That's not what I meant. All I mean—"

Emily walked out the door.

"That's it," Ford told the teacher. He nodded at the woman in the white lab coat. "You're up."

"Well, thank you, Mr. Carson," the teacher said. "Let's— well, yes—let's give Mr. Carson a round of applause."

A few of the kids obliged. Bailey continued erasing his desk.

Ford left the classroom, expecting Emily to accost him in the hall. But she wasn't there. He made his way to the parking lot, thinking maybe he'd find her outside. But the parking lot was empty too.


Ford nursed his hangover at the studio with coffee and a fried egg. The struggle eventually paid off when he discovered that the White Elephant's EP, *he do the police in different voices*, had been the original title for T.S. Eliot's poem, *The Waste Land*. The album's five tracks corresponded with the poem's five parts.

"Dear Mrs. Equitone," the record's opening number, borrowed a selection of lines from the poem's opening section,

"The Burial of the Dead." With this new understanding, the singer's previously impenetrable vocals became more decipherable. Still, it took Ford nearly an hour to piece together the song's lyrics. The chorus thrilled him: *Mrs. Equitone / Dear Equitone / I bring the horoscope / One must be so careful these days.*

Ford spent the next three days transcribing the jumbled lyrics for all five songs. The second track, "Hurry Up Please," was his favorite. Despite its title, the number was a slow, moody piece with scrappy guitars, a thunderous floor tom, and an expansive organ. Listening to it was like walking in the rain; it got heavier the farther you went. The chorus—which wasn't really a chorus but more like an extension of the verse—bookended the song. The singer slurred: *The wind under the door / Do you know nothing? / Do you see nothing? / Hurry up please / What's that noise?*

Ford's phone rang, showing Emily's name. She called to confirm he had received her email about the shellfish. He told her he had. Nevertheless, Emily went back over the information.

"*One must be so careful these days,*" Ford said, quoting Eliot.

"He'll tell you I'm being overly cautious," Emily said.

Ford could hear the uncertainty in her response. She couldn't tell if he was patronizing her with his previous remark. But she certainly wasn't going to accuse him of it. She rarely accused him of anything these days.

He continued with the impromptu game, scrolling through the poem's lines on his laptop. "*I never know what you're thinking,*" he said, regretting the choice immediately.

"Excuse me?" she asked.

There was no sense in turning back. "*Do you know nothing? Do you see nothing? Do you remember nothing?*" Ford recited the lines.

"What's wrong with you?"

He finally cracked.

"*The Waste Land,*" he said. "I've been working on a piece inspired by *The Waste Land*. It's a T.S. Eliot poem."

"I know *The Waste Land,*" she said.

"You've read it?" he asked.

She was silent.

"Emily?"

"*Between the conception / And the creation / Between the emotion / And the response / Falls the shadow.*"

"Is that from *The Waste Land*?" he asked, not remembering the lines.

"My tattoo," she said sharply.

He'd forgotten all about the stanza on her ribcage. She'd had it done her sophomore year. He hated it from day one. The tattoo felt like a direct challenge. An assertion that things were changing—that she was changing—and there was nothing he could do about it.

"What section is that in?" he asked, scrolling through the poem.

"It's not from *The Waste Land,*" she said. "It's from *The Hollow Men.*"

Ford leaned back in his chair. "That's another of his?"

"Have you blocked out everything?"

Ford hesitated. "Not *everything.*"

"I'd planned to write my honors thesis on Eliot," she reminded him.

"That I remember," he lied.

They were both silent.

"I've been reading his poem all week," he told her. "I don't understand half of it, but I like it all the same."

"How's Bailey's piece coming?" she asked.

Ford eyed the canvas. He'd painted the words *The Suburbs* across it, hopeful that something, anything, on the stretched fabric might propel the project forward.

"I hit a wall," he confessed, surprised by the admission.

"You've got time," she assured him.

"It'll get finished," he said defensively.

She was silent, before saying, "*One must be so careful these days.*"

He laughed through his nose, realizing then that he hadn't had a drink since discovering the connection between the album and the poem. He counted off the number of days on his hand. All fingers up but his pinky. That's how he knew a project was working. When he was so absorbed that he didn't need anything else. He loved that feeling.

"*I will show you fear in a handful of dust,*" Emily said. "That was my favorite line from *The Waste Land*. Do you remember me reciting it to you that day on the beach? I kept scooping up the sand and easing it out of my hand and repeating the phrase. You got so frustrated because I wouldn't tell you where it was from or why I kept saying it."

She paused. "I'm not sure why I was acting that way toward you," she said.

Ford didn't remember the episode.

They were silent.

"Listen," she said, "I'm not trying to be overbearing. But can you please respond to my emails? I'll try and be mindful and not send too many. But I get anxious. You know how I am."

Ford agreed to be more prompt. She thanked him. They ended things on a good note.

# CHAPTER 8

Ford merged onto the highway. A halo circled the moon, transforming the satellite into the sky's lone pupil. He and Grace hadn't spoken all week. But unlike with her previous silences, he didn't worry. He hadn't the time to. He had nailed down the basic concept for her collage: a chessboard floating in the water with a mound of sand in the center and a little girl sledding down it. On some of the board's outer squares would stand figures: Tiresias, the old man with wrinkled breasts; Mrs. Equitone and Madame Sosostris; the Phoenician sailor; the Hanged Man; Albert and Lil; dogs and rats. He didn't yet know what most of these characters would look like, but he knew he'd find them in old medical journals or dictionaries or postcards or hardback copies of *Reader's Digest*.

Ford admired the sky's bright eye. The distraction nearly caused a collision. He slammed on the brakes. The highway was a parking lot. The standstill lasted for half an hour before the traffic inched along. Around the bend, Ford spotted the distant emergency lights. Cars in the left lane merged into the right, taking the off-ramp.

Twenty minutes later, Ford followed suit. Hunger and proximity lured him to Eden's. He hadn't been to the strip club in months. The old brick building stood between a former tattoo parlor and a small three-seat barbershop. Eden's marquee advertised $9.99 Friday night steaks.

Noire smiled when she saw him sitting at his usual spot in the back corner.

"Ford Odyssey," she said, revealing her crooked front tooth. "Thought for sure I was gonna find your picture on a milk carton."

"I thought you were lactose intolerant."

"Didn't say I was gonna buy the milk carton," she said.

He smiled in surrender.

"You still a whiskey man or would you rather I bring you some milk?"

"Only if the carton's got my face on it," he said.

She nodded and headed for the bar.

The stage split the room. Stools lined around it. Most were occupied. A middle-aged couple sat at one of the nearby two tops. Meanwhile, a group of young guys gathered at the bar for shots. Noire slid past them with Ford's whiskey on her tray.

"This one's on the house," she said, joining him at the table. "And the next one too. And the next one after that."

"You trying to get me pregnant?" he asked.

"I *am* pregnant," Noire said. "And don't go asking about the father now either. Tell you this much, though, he's not keen on my decision to keep it. Thought I was stupid from the get-go. Thought he met him a nice, dumb country girl he could keep on the side. Not that I was planning this. But I know child support'll cost him a lot less than a divorce."

"Congratulations?"

She shrugged. "I'm leaving town. Tomorrow's my last night. And see now you must have sensed my departure and felt compelled to bid me farewell. Sweet man that you are."

"Where you headed?"

"Franklin-fucking-Tennessee. Back with Mom. Figure I'll write him once I get there. Get me a P.O. box or something, so I don't have to worry about him trying to find me."

She rubbed her flat stomach.

"How crazy am I?" she asked, looking at her midsection. "I left Tennessee for one man and now I'm heading back there to get away from another." She shook her head. "But God let there be another man inside me now. If this here turns out a girl, Lord knows I'll be paying. Me and Mom had us some battles back in the day. She's the reason I left Tennessee in the first place."

"Thought you left for a man."

"Well, hell," she said, conceding the fact. "Sure. But when is anything ever that simple?"

Noire touched her stomach again, studying it once more. "You've always worn nice shoes, you know that Ford Mustang?" She looked up at him and smiled. "That's how I knew I liked you. Most men come in here talking big but they're wearing nasty sneakers, so you know whatever they're holding is all they've got. Not you, though. I remember when you first come in here. You were wearing a nice pair of brown leather shoes. And you were all quiet-like, watching the girls from this very table, sipping that very drink, and I remember thinking, I like this man."

Noire rested her chin in the palm of her hand. When her elbow slipped off the table, her teeth nearly crashed into it. She laughed.

"How much have you had?" Ford asked.

Her eyes watered. "I'm scared," she said. "Thought maybe a sip would help figure things out. That's how I decided on going home. He's high profile, this man. If I said his name your eyes would explode."

She waved off the statement. "That ain't true. That's just how big he's got in my mind. He lives in South Carolina. You believe that? Drives all this way to avoid getting caught. You'd figure if you're gonna come all this way, why not go to Charlotte? Tits are a lot perkier in those parts.

"But he said he liked me," she continued. "Then he said he *loved* me. Every time we'd end up together he'd cry himself a big old storm saying he couldn't stand it, how much he loved me. But I sure didn't love him. And I don't think he really loved me. I think he just wanted to think he did. He's got religion. And I think thinking he loved me somehow made it all better in his head. And then this happened and so I text him and a few minutes later I get this call from a number I don't know and when I don't answer, it keeps calling. Until by the third go-around I pick up and it's him and he's just angry as all hell, asking if I'm stupid or something? He starts yelling, why the hell would you ever text something like that? Are you stupid? And then he says to me that I better never contact him again. That he won't say what he'll do but I can be certain it'll get done. That sort of thing. And so now here I am, a little drunk with this man's baby inside me, talking with you about it, and all because you wear nice shoes. It's funny, isn't it Ford Explorer? How these things happen?"

They shared a cigarette in the parking lot. Ford didn't normally smoke, but he figured he'd do the kid inside her a favor. She asked if raising a baby would be hard. Ford told her it usually was. She pressed into him, resting the side of her face against his chest. He rubbed her back. Noire looked up at him and smiled, almost bashful. She then stood on her toes and kissed him. He leaned down to help.

"We could and I'd let you," she said, "but maybe this right here is better than all that."

Ford nodded. "I'm seeing someone anyway."

"Well, aren't you a dog," she said, still in his arms.

"Probably."

"You gonna come back and see me off tomorrow?"

"Not if it leads to more of this."

"A neutered dog," she teased.

He nodded again.

"What if I promised only to give you one more of these tomorrow and nothing else," she said, tapping his lips with her finger. "There's nothing wrong with that, is there? A neutered dog can still kiss, can't he?"

"You shouldn't be drinking," he said.

"Tonight's my last."

"Shouldn't be smoking, either."

"The baby'll have to deal with that a little longer, I'm guessing."

"You'll be a good mother," Ford said.

"I hope it's a boy."

"I bet it is."

They continued to hold each other.

"I'm betting you're a better father than you give yourself credit for."

He didn't remember ever talking with her about Bailey, but he supposed he must have.

"He'll be here in a few weeks."

"I'll be gone," she said. "But you'd have brought him here to meet me, now wouldn't you? If I weren't leaving?"

"I would."

She smiled. "You're full of shit."

Before he could pretend otherwise, she said, "But that's nice of you to say."

Noire rested her head against his chest, squeezing him. "Tell me something else that's nice."

"You'll make a wonderful mother."

"Only if it's a boy," she said. "God, let it be a boy."

"You'll be wonderful no matter what," he told her.

She cried.

Ford kissed the top of her head. She was a sweet girl. It made him sad to think nothing good would ever come her way.

At home he deliberated for nearly an hour before texting Grace. He kept the message formal in case JR screened her calls. Not that it mattered. Still, Ford liked the idea of keeping JR guessing. He wrote:

> *I've made some great progress on your collage. I'd really love to speak with you about it. I don't want to miss anything. Your input matters to me. Talk to you soon.*

The alcohol made his text seem wildly romantic and mysterious in its coded and suggestive language. But the moment he hit send, the delivered words turned stiff and potentially alienating.

Ford checked his phone compulsively, fixing himself two additional drinks while awaiting a response. But a response never came.

He stepped outside into the chilly November air to watch his neighbor watch television. The guy never turned it off. The man would die alone inside his home to a thunderous laugh track.

Leaves shuffled in the darkness. Ford held his breath and listened. The world around him fell unnaturally quiet. His eyes adjusted, but he saw nothing. He cleared his throat. If it were an animal it would have run off at the sound. Instead, silence. He cleared his throat again.

Nothing.

"Hey!" he shouted.

A light breeze stirred the trees. The wind, he told himself, laughing. But he could hear his effort. He laughed some more to cover it up. The wind, he tried reassuring himself.

Inside, Ford killed the lights and made his way through the house, pausing at each window. *There's nothing out there. It's all in your head.*

He checked his phone once more for a response. It was three in the morning. *She's asleep, you idiot. Go to bed.*

By sunrise, she had still not replied. Nor did she respond that afternoon. Her silence tainted the project. He couldn't get back into Eliot's words. He wasted the entire day checking his phone.

That evening, Ford left the studio with an older piece inspired by the Tinman Yates song "Apple Seeker." He planned to give it to Noire as a farewell gift.

"She called out," the cocktail waitress told him.

"Called out?" he shouted over the music.

The cocktail waitress nodded.

"Well, what'd she say?"

"They called me in, that's all I know," she said, tapping her pen against her writing pad.

Ford ordered a drink.

A dancer spun her way down the center pole just as a curtain whisked open to the right of the stage. A man stormed out. Across the room, the club's lone bouncer stood from his stool, eyeing the man as he marched out of Eden's.

The cocktail waitress returned with Ford's drink.

"Noire was a friend," he told her. He didn't know why he said this. The woman didn't care either way. "I was coming to say goodbye."

"Maybe try tomorrow."

"Tonight was supposed to be her last night."

"Which one is she?"

"Short girl with brown hair," he said. "From Tennessee."

"Is she the black chick?"

"No."

"Why she call herself Noire?"

Ford realized he didn't know Noire's actual name. "She had the Bob Dylan lyrics tattooed on her back shoulder," he said. "Real skinny. Dark eyes."

"All I know is someone called out," she said, looking around the room for a way out.

"But do you know who I'm talking about?"

"I only just started last month."

Ford thanked her for the drink.

The next dancer spread her legs at the front of the stage. A man stood with a dollar bill in his teeth. The dancer insisted he deliver the tip without using his hands. The crowd laughed as the man tried his best to make the transaction. He nudged, turned, and twisted before practically spitting the dollar on her. The dancer clapped as if the soiled bill amused her. She then took the man's fat baldhead and placed him between her breasts. The room erupted. The man smiled broadly when she was through with him.

Ford scanned the club, hoping he might find Noire hidden in a corner. Instead, he spotted JR alongside the stage, smiling with the rest of the crowd. Ford checked his phone. Grace still hadn't replied to his previous text.

"You want another?" the cocktail waitress asked.

Her appearance startled Ford.

"I know that man," he said, pointing at JR. But JR was gone. Ford searched the room. JR pushed open the door, exiting the club.

"Where you going?" the cocktail waitress called after Ford.

He paused, taking out a twenty and pressing it into her hand. "If you hear anything about Noire, you let me know."

"I don't know anything."

"*If*," Ford repeated.

She studied the twenty, calculating the tip versus the request. "I don't even know who you are," she said.

Outside, the parking lot stood empty. Ford had no plan but felt an opportunity lost. An eighteen-wheeler sped past. A cold gust from its tires reached him. He turned his back on the wind. Near the club's door, a woman stared him down. He didn't recognize her at first. She wore a blonde wig. The woman approached Ford as if she'd been expecting him, pressing into his body just as Noire had the previous night.

"You're okay," he told her.

"I'm freezing," Grace said.

"What are you doing here?" he asked.

"What are *you* doing here?"

"The same as everyone else," Ford said.

"I'm freezing," she repeated.

They took separate cars. She rode his bumper the entire way. But there was a moment on the bridge over the French Broad River where he thought she might turn around. Her headlights shrank from his mirror. He slowed down near the middle of the bridge but made it a point to avoid touching his brakes. His car nearly came to a stop before she raced toward him, her headlights on his bumper the rest of the way.

# CHAPTER 9

He packed dryer lint beneath the logs to ensure the fire would catch. He then lit a match and watched it soar, closing the black mesh curtain. Grace waited for him on the rug with pillows and a blanket from the bedroom. He joined her. Neither mentioned Eden's. They lay together on the floor, watching the flames.

"I'm so tired," Grace said, her body curled into his.

Ford massaged her lower back. "Sleep."

"I can't stop thinking."

Ford continued massaging her.

"I keep going over things," she said, rubbing her forehead. "Why do we do that? Why do we always assume there's a causal relationship?"

Ford ran his fingers up her spine, pausing on her shoulders before pressing into her neck.

"That feels good," she said.

"You should try and sleep."

"I can't," she said. "I can't stop thinking."

"Then tell me what you're thinking about," he said.

"I don't even know where to begin."

"How about Houston."

"What about Houston?"

"I still don't know how you ended up there."

She and her mother returned to Texas shortly after the Chelsea incident. Rather than settle in Chappell Hill, which was her mother's hometown, Nancy opted for Houston, where an old friend helped land Grace a scholarship to Winston High.

Soon after their arrival, Nancy found God. But even God could not help her cope with all that she had witnessed in Yellow Springs. She kept Grace indoors except for school and church. Through God, Nancy continued mining answers. She had Grace fast. Then she had Grace pray and bathe three times a day. Then she had Grace drink only whole milk. Then she had Grace listen to conservative talk radio.

"Why are you doing this?" Grace would ask.

"To save you," her mother would say.

"I don't need to be saved."

"God will be the judge of that."

"God doesn't care if I'm a lesbian."

"Drink your milk."

"Milk comes from the tit of a female cow."

"Why do you insist on hurting me? Why are you and your father so cruel?"

"You're cruel," Grace said.

"God will determine that."

"Is God a man or a woman?" Grace asked.

"Watch your mouth."

"I'm asking."

"God is a man," her mother said.

"Then what are you worried about?" Grace asked.

"I worry about your eternal salvation."

"Because you think I'm a lesbian?"

Her mother insisted Grace drink the glass of milk.

"Don't you get it," Grace said. "If God is a man, what makes you think he's any different from the rest of them?"

"You're not making any sense."

"That's because you aren't listening," Grace said. "You never do. If God's a man, then there's nothing he likes more than a pair of pink pussies."

Nancy took her daughter's glass of milk and poured it down the drain.

The school therapist encouraged Grace to join one of the athletic teams. Grace figured if she was going to be outdoors in eastern Texas, she might as well stay cool. Though far from a gifted swimmer, she had an innate talent for diving, which was how she landed a spot on the team.

Grace hardly spoke to her teammates, much less the boy swimmers. But Jeffrey soon caught her eye. She was taken by his butterfly stroke, which she thought magnificent if not impossible. She hadn't a competitive bone in her body, yet it was difficult not to appreciate the perfection of Jeffery's aquatic movements. He elevated out of the water like some mythological sea creature. His massive wingspan always made it look as if his emerging hands would get caught in the line floats. Every so often Grace found herself wishing for it, certain his strength would simply snap the lines or pull them up and out of the water. She wanted to see it happen.

The two made eye contact for the first time from across the pool. He was on the diving board. She sat on a vinyl strapped chaise lounge with her head sideways, hoping gravity would pull the chlorinated water from her ear. His look was not salacious but his attention did linger. As did hers. Until finally, with the hope to impress, he darted from the back of the board to its loose front, taking an assertive bounce, only to smack the surface of the water with his belly at the exact moment warm liquid oozed out of Grace's ear canal.


Her father called that winter. Their first exchange since Grace and her mother relocated to Houston. She wasn't sure how he got their number. And she wasn't sure if his latest attack had been prepared in advance (perhaps even rehearsed) or simply inspired by her voice. Whatever the case, she could practically smell the alcohol through the receiver.

He addressed her as his *little dyke*. Then his *sweet, little dyke*. Then his *sweet, little dyke who ran her off*.

"I'm hanging up," Grace managed to say.

"I'll kill myself," Dr. Hudson threatened. "I've got a gun. If you hang up, I'll kill myself."

Her anger, which only moments before ran through her like static, subsided. She stared into the hallway mirror at an empty, unloving gaze.

"You don't have a gun," she said.

"Yes, I do."

"Then let's hear it."

Her father laughed.

"You lie," she said.

"My heartless, little dyke," he groaned. "Imagine if that was the last thing you said to me."

"You lie," she repeated.

"My cruel, heartless, little dyke."

"I'm not a fucking dyke," she said. "And if I was, I wouldn't be *your* dyke."

"You took her from me."

"So kill yourself."

"You and your mother both," he said.

There was a long pause. For a moment, she doubted herself. Maybe he did have a gun. But instead of a pop, her father began to weep. She'd never heard him cry before. Indistinguishable epithets broke through stymied and stuttered breaths, swallowed by additional bouts of inconsolable tears.

She wanted to feel something. That was the worst part. She sat there listening, waiting for her mind or body to react. But everything stayed inside her, locked away. Or simply missing.

"You'll be fine," she told him, and hung up the phone.


Grace took a taxi to the beach. Because of the distance and her age, the driver required a flat rate up-front. Short ten bucks, she offered the driver a blowjob. He guffawed, then told her to get in. When she reached for the front handle, he directed her

126

with his thumb to the back. Every so often he'd look her over in the rearview mirror and shake his head. She could tell part of him wanted it. They all did. But another part of her knew nothing was going to happen.

As the city disappeared behind them, Grace thought of her father. She imagined his body on the floor, part of his brain somewhere on the wall behind him. The more she contemplated the image, the more absurd it became. Her mother had been right. He really was just a delusional, pathetic, and desperate fraud.

Heavy gray clouds enveloped the sky. The beach was empty. "You got on a lot of layers," the cab driver observed through the rearview mirror. It was the first and only thing he said to her since they'd started the drive.

"You want me to take them off?" Grace asked. Her words sounded foreign. None of this was real, she thought.

He turned around, eyeing her for a moment. "This here's your stop," he said.

Seagulls swirled above the shoreline. The brown, murky water crashed below. A few fishermen cast lines from a distant pier. An unseen runner left footprints behind in the sand.

Grace kept her shoes on as she entered the water. The same went for her three t-shirts, two sweaters, two pairs of pants and jacket. A lone pelican landed on the shore and watched the cold ocean gradually claim her.

Once absorbed, instinct kicked in. Grace tried to swim. But it was pointless. Her clothing had turned to cement. She couldn't lift her arms and could just barely kick her legs. But it wasn't enough to satisfy her sudden, dreadful urge to live. She kicked again; the water continued its pull.

She thought about her mother. Where would Nancy go? And who would Nancy turn into next? What new religion might she follow? What new profession might she pursue? Who had her mother ever truly been?

Then another thought struck. What if her body never washed ashore? What if the ocean kept her? Would her mother remain a prisoner to Texas, held by the false hope of her daughter's eventual return?

Grace felt her body giving out, her breath nearly gone. She thought of her mother asleep in their former home in Yellow Springs. Her father's home. She thought of Dr. Hudson sitting in his reading chair. A book in one hand, a glass of whiskey in the other. He wasn't a good father, but maybe some just weren't.

Her legs gave out. She began to sink. And then, without explanation, she surged. A violent ejection from the water. The smack of cold air across her wet face. Her lungs gasping for oxygen. A single arm hooked around her waist. Her limp body pulled ashore and released onto the wet sand where she coughed violently, lungs afire.

When she managed her breath and opened her eyes, Jeffrey Burnett hovered above her.

"You okay?" he asked.

She vomited. The ocean washed it away. The lone pelican remained on the beach, its small eyes on Grace. Jeffrey helped her up just as a gust of wind nearly pulled out her legs. Grace leaned into him. Particles of sand pelleted her face. Despite the assault, she kept her eyes open, watching the pelican's still, silent stance.

Across the street, Jeffrey guided her up the back stairs of a lime green beach house. Since he was eleven, Jeffrey told her, he spent his winter breaks here. He liked training in the ocean. He enjoyed the challenge of the current and the cold water and the empty beaches that came with gloomy December days. And he cherished the solitude and time away from his four older siblings. And he appreciated that his mother trusted him enough to stay there alone. And he didn't mind that nobody else in his family seemed to notice his absence. He shared all of this with Grace while the two still ascended the stairs.

Inside, he helped her undress. Layer after wet layer. When she got down to her final shirt and pants, he pointed toward the bathroom. "There's a bathrobe in there if you'd like."

She finished undressing under the glow of the sink's florescent light, too tired to rinse the sand out of her hair. She pulled the bathrobe from the door's back hanger. When she reemerged, Jeffrey was in the process of loading the washing machine with her clothes. She was too tired to retrieve the final layer, which she left behind on the bathroom floor.

He directed her to the couch and brought her a glass of Gatorade. "Electrolytes," he said, before leaving to gather her wet pants, shirt, underwear, and bra from the bathroom. She was too tired to apologize. She sipped from the glass and watched him close the lid to the washing machine.

"I usually have a few corndogs for lunch," he told her. "If you want, I can make you one."

She nodded and he nodded back.

They watched reruns of *The Simpsons* until the wash cycle finished. Jeffrey then transferred the laundry into the dryer, pausing to ask her if any items needed to be line dried.

She couldn't initially respond. The question somehow gutted her. Who was this considerate boy who saved her?

"No," she finally spoke.

By the time her clothes dried, it was close to dinner. He offered to order them a pizza.

"You eat like shit," she said.

He smiled proudly.

"I should call my mom," she said.

He brought her the cordless.

"I don't know what to tell her," she said.

"I'd offer to drive you home but I don't have a car."

"Do you even have a license?"

"Driver's permit."

"Maybe I'll call her after the pizza," Grace said.

They ate slices of cheese and pepperoni and watched reruns of *Seinfeld*. Grace had yet to change back into her clothes. Jeffrey folded them into a neat stack on a nearby recliner. Even with the carbs and electrolytes, she was too tired to move. Too tired to worry about her mother. Too tired to think.

By nightfall, she remained in Jeffrey's bathrobe.

"Are you going to get in trouble?" he asked.

She wanted to laugh, but she hadn't the strength. "I'm not leaving this couch," she said.

He studied her. "I'm Jeffrey, by the way," he said.

This time she did laugh. "I know who you are."

"I know," he said. "I just thought—well, in case you didn't, I guess."

"Well, then I'm Grace," she said.

"I know," he said.

They were both silent.

"How'd you even find me out there?" she asked.

"I spotted you from the balcony," he said, pointing at the sliding glass door.

She studied what little she could see of the outdoor deck. The night concealed the ocean. Still, she tried to imagine what she must have looked like. A bundle of clothes waddling out to sea. She eyed the folded stack of jeans, sweaters, shirts, and jacket. Her accomplices in a failed suicide attempt.

"I won't say anything," he said.

On the screen, Kramer slid through Jerry's apartment door.

"Do you like *The Sopranos*?" he asked.

"I don't know what that is," she said.

The entire room was dark, except for the screen. His teeth reflected its light. "I recorded the entire first season," he said, standing up. "You want ice cream?"

"God, you really do eat like shit."

"Is that a yes?"

She exhaled as if the decision was a great burden. She tried to imagine what it would be like to fall in love with this boy. Could love be premeditated? She'd always thought it had to hit you like a giant wave. If she did decide to fall in love with him, when would he change? Was it inevitable that all boys had to become terrible men? Was she herself not something terrible?

"Do you think you're special?" she asked. "Because you saved me?"

"No," he said, as if he'd long been anticipating the question.

"There could be someone else out there right now," she said, pointing toward the back patio. "You gonna save us all?"

"No, I don't think so," he answered.

"I could have pulled you under, you know?"

"And I could have just let you drown," he reminded her.

"But you wouldn't have," she said. "How many times have you stood out there just hoping for the chance to save some sweet, stupid girl from drowning?"

"Honestly," he said, "I thought you were a crazy homeless person."

Again, she laughed. "Do you always talk this way?" she asked.

"I don't know," he said. "I guess I never gave it much thought."

"But you aren't stupid," she said.

"Did you think I was?"

"I don't know," she said. "You're very kind."

132

"You shouldn't mistake the two."

"I'm just curious what makes you snap."

"When my blood sugar level gets low," he said. "So do you want some ice cream or not?"

She took her time to respond, wanting to see this other side of him. To get a glimpse into their future. He remained still. A commercial break momentarily darkened the room. She was a terrible person, she thought. How could she not be?

The screen lit back up. He was alone here, she reminded herself. The thought excited her. He was alone. This kind, patient boy. This sweet, stupid would-be man. He was alone.

She wanted to know everything about him. Every last eccentric detail. Certain there were many, but equally certain he would reveal none. Which only made him more intriguing. Was this love? The desire to discover another person's secrets. But what happens once you figure them all out? Is that why it never lasts? Because there are only so many secrets to surprise a person with. Or was that true love? The ability to outlast shock.

"What are my options?" she asked.

"Ultimate Neapolitan."

"What does that mean?"

He smiled. "Chocolate, vanilla, and strawberry."

"Not vanilla," she said.

"Which side of the container do you want then?" he asked.

"I'll have whatever you're having."

"I'm having all three."

133

"Then I'll have all three minus the vanilla."

"You like to be difficult, don't you?"

She was still just fifteen but had never felt quite so young. And up until that moment, she'd never felt quite so old, either.

He brought her back a bowl of strawberry and chocolate ice cream. As she scooped her first bite, he removed a VHS from below the television, feeding the tape into the VCR. He then rejoined her on the couch, placing his bowl of vanilla, strawberry, and chocolate ice cream on his lap. She rested her head against his shoulder. Jeffrey slurped his dessert. Images of New Jersey flashed across the screen.

She was only fifteen, she thought again. But she already knew. This sweet, stupid boy had no idea who he let inside his home. The only thing that made it fair, she supposed, was that she had no idea what sort of home she'd stepped into.

Shortly after winter break, Jeffrey introduced Grace to his best friend George. George made mixtapes, which in 2002 was a dying art. He had an eclectic taste in music that spanned decades: Roy Orbison, The Ramones, Madonna, Prince, David Bowie, Outkast, Rancid, Queen.

"I don't subscribe to genres," George told Grace, handing her the first of many cassettes.

The diverse collection of songs accompanied a diverse period of nicknames for George. He'd disliked his birth name long before George W. Bush was elected, he told her. But the president made it ever the more challenging to deal with. He insisted Jeffrey and Grace call him Geo, followed by Ore, followed by his middle name Frederick, followed by Fred, followed by Rick, followed by G, followed by Geo again before finally accepting the fact that none of the nicknames would stick—that they'd always slip and call him George.

Once Jeffrey got his license, the three spent their Friday nights listening to George's mixtapes while cruising in Jeffrey's 2002 Lexus LX. For a period, they stole lawn ornaments from the Montrose and Greater Heights neighborhoods. Unsure what to do with the loot, they eventually settled on relocating their collection to the wealthiest homes in River Oaks. The ritual made them laugh: the thought of some CEO discovering the weathered face of a ceramic gnome tainting his otherwise pristine lawn.

But then one day it all stopped.

"We're a bunch of hypocrites," George said from the car's back seat. "Acting like we're not the kids of these CEOs. Shit JR, you live in River Oaks. We're a bunch of rich hypocrites stealing gnomes in a Lexus."

"Speak for yourself," Grace said.

"Oh please," George objected, hovering over the center console. "You're practically a Burnett at this point. Two years and I've never even met your mother."

"That's by design," Grace said.

"So mysterious," George teased, his outrage gone.

"Nothing mysterious about it," Grace said. "She's just a crazy bitch. And a Jesus freak on top of that."

"Well, now I'm even more intrigued."

Jeffrey pointed out a gnome on a nearby lawn. He pulled over, turning down the radio and killing the headlights. "We doing this?" he asked.

"JR, don't try and change the subject," George said.

"Maybe Grace doesn't want to talk about it," Jeffrey said.

"Now you're both just teasing me," George said. "You two have me as hard as a rock with all this mystery."

"You've got issues," Jeffrey said.

George withdrew to the back seat. "I do, don't I?" he asked in a hollow tone.

"Oh boy," Jeffrey said, shifting the car into park. He turned to face George. "We can't legally adopt you yet," he reminded him, hoping to get a laugh.

"Don't worry, I'm not looking for fatherly advice," George said, unamused.

Jeffrey eyed Grace for help.

"If we're gonna do this we should do it," she said. "Someone might call the cops if they see us just sitting here."

"Let them call the fucking cops," George said. "We're a bunch a rich, white babies in a fucking Lexus. They'd suck our dicks."

"I don't have a dick," Grace reminded him.

"Don't be gross," Jeffrey said, looking out the driver side window.

"God you're such a choir boy," George told Jeffrey.

"I am not."

"No, I love it," George said. "We all do. You belong in like Wisconsin in 1951."

"And you belong on a seesaw," Jeffrey said.

"Huh?" Grace asked.

"His mood swings," Jeffrey said. "The ups and downs."

George burst with laughter. "Oh my God, JR. You're already telling dad jokes. You're fucking adorable. Adopt me already."

The three laughed, although Grace could sense Jeffrey's unease. He didn't mind being the butt of the joke. That was the dynamic since Grace turned the former duet into a trio. But often when he and Grace were alone, Jeffrey would ask if she thought George had ill feelings toward him. Why was he always so mean? Grace would defend George, insisting that he hadn't been mean. That Jeffrey was being too sensitive. That George had just been joking. And sometimes that would work. Jeffrey would snap out of it and let go. But just as often Jeffrey would stay silent or lock himself inside the downstairs bathroom.

Back in the car, Jeffrey said, "Be a good boy and go steal us that gnome so we can get back to being a bunch of no-good hypocrites."

But George didn't budge. "No," he said. "I don't think I want to steal gnomes anymore."

They soon saw less of George. Occasionally, he'd come back around and spend a weekend with them, but it wasn't the same. It felt obligatory. And he was often distracted. His eyes

137

constantly scanned whatever crowd they were in. Jeffrey eventually confronted George about this, worried his friend was on drugs. George laughed, saying wouldn't that be nice.

Rumors started around school. Someone claimed they saw George holding hands with another boy. Jeffrey defended George in his absence. Said people didn't know what they were talking about. Called it bullshit. Insisted anyone who repeated the lie was the true faggot. But nothing seemed to stop the rumor from spreading.

One afternoon, Grace and Jeffrey ran into George at Black Hole, a local coffeehouse. George said, "I hear there's been a lot of talk."

They didn't know how to respond. George's eyes watered. He started shaking his head violently. He said, "Well, it's not like there's anything I can do about it."

Jeffrey began telling George that it didn't mean anything. That people were dumb. And for a moment Grace saw hope in George's eyes. But as Jeffrey continued on about setting the record straight, George's hope vanished.

"It's probably Goalie Greg spreading all this," Jeffrey said. "Trying to cover his own tracks. You know he blew some kid from the Woodlands' soccer team? That's what Carl and Mikey told me at practice the other day."

George nodded, numb and silent, because what else could he do?

A week later he was gone, shipped off to a boarding school somewhere in Colorado. Of course, by then everyone knew, even Jeffrey. His initial shock quickly turned to anger.

He had stood up for George. And all the while George had been lying to him.

"I can't believe you're making this about you," Grace said.

"We were friends."

"And you guys still *are* friends."

Jeffrey huffed.

"Oh what? You don't like him now because he's gay?"

"I don't want to think about it."

"Think about what?"

"I don't know," Jeffrey said. "It's just all really weird."

"George is gay," Grace said. "And people are being assholes about it. You're being an asshole about it. He's your friend. And he's my friend. And him being gay doesn't change that."

"He should have told me."

"Why?" Grace asked. "So he could witness firsthand you being a complete dick about it?"

"I'm not trying to be a dick."

"Well, you are."

"I'm sorry," Jeffery said.

"You should be."

They paused, neither sure what to say next. They rarely fought.

"And just so you know, we're still adopting him," Grace said.

139

Jeffrey laughed. "Sure we are."

But the experience changed him. At school, Jeffrey distanced himself from George, despite George's absence. And so George became *faggot this* and *faggot that* whenever his name came up.

Though Grace hated Jeffrey for doing this, she could also now love him more because of it. His behavior mitigated her deep sense of guilt. For years, Jeffrey had no idea who she had been in Yellow Springs—no idea about Chelsea or the sad, angry boys. And now she didn't have to feel bad about keeping this from him. Because based on his reaction to George's outing, Jeffrey could never know. Not if they wanted to continue to love each other.

"Everything happened so fast," Grace told Ford.

They remained on the floor, watching the flames slowly crumble the logs.

"And then it was over," she said. "Everyone moved on. Except no one ever really moves on. Everyone pretends the past is the past and will remain in the past so long as we keep calling it the past. But then the past comes back. It always comes back."

To prove her point, she returned to the past once more. Only this time she didn't travel nearly as far back, opting instead for a story that occurred just a few months prior.

Jeffrey invited Georgia out for a drink in Sugar Land. He arrived early, surprised by how nervous the meeting had him.

He ordered a scotch. On his second round he heard his name. He didn't recognize the woman standing behind his barstool. In his mind he'd expected something far less refined. Admittedly, he was shocked by how much his friend looked like a woman. No trace of facial hair, no sign of an Adam's apple, and breasts held in a tight red dress revealing a curvy frame.

Throughout the night, as the two friends caught up, Jeffrey noticed other men glancing in Georgia's direction. At first he found it all a little strange. Here he was with his former best friend, a man he hadn't seen in over a decade, and yet they spoke as if they'd just gotten back from stealing gnomes. Only now his former friend was a woman.

Jeffrey told Georgia about his job.

"I don't really follow sports," Georgia said. "But I did listen to your show the other day. Your voice is much deeper on-air."

Jeffrey smiled. "E-nun-ci-a-tion," he said. "It's not about tone or volume. It's all about e-nun-ci-a-tion."

"Well, you enunciate things very well."

Jeffrey updated Georgia on Grace.

"Kids?" Georgia asked.

"No," Jeffrey said.

They both sipped their drinks.

"She didn't want to join us?" Georgia asked.

The question reminded Jeffrey why he arranged the meeting in the first place. He didn't know where to begin. So he rambled. Georgia listened, searching Jeffrey's eyes for indication of where all this was headed. And then it arrived. First the confession about how he had distanced himself from George when the rumors were confirmed those many years ago. Followed by how sorry he was for his failure as a friend; that he hated how things ended between them; that he hated the way everyone had treated him.

Georgia continued to nod, looking around the place before pausing on the mirror behind the bar. She fixed her hair. "I had a feeling that's what this might be about," she said.

"I wanted to apologize."

"I got that," Georgia said. "You felt bad."

"I did."

"And now you feel better, I bet."

"I wanted to apologize," Jeffrey repeated.

"And what a nice place to apologize at." Georgia pulled a menu from behind the napkin stand and read the restaurant's name aloud. "At Teresa's Greek Bistro."

"I figured . . ."

"You figured?"

"I wanted to apologize," Jeffrey repeated.

"Yes, you've made that point fairly clear," Georgia said. "And maybe that's my cue. That I need to spell things out."

Jeffrey straightened in his stool.

"What's the matter?" Georgia asked.

"I was slipping," he said. "Too much scotch."

"Oh, the alcohol," Georgia said.

"Yeah, the alcohol."

"You don't see it, do you?"

"See what?"

"Your apology," she said. "That's not what this is."

Jeffrey finished his drink. "Whatever you're trying to suggest—"

"*Suggest?*" she said.

"Yeah," he said. "I came here to apologize. That's all."

"You've told me this now about fifteen times."

"And you're trying to act like that isn't the case. Well, whatever you're thinking, you can stop."

"You're unbelievable."

"The check," Jeffrey called to the bartender.

Georgia placed her hand on Jeffrey's leg.

"What the fuck are you doing?"

"Your leg," she said, letting it go. "You keep shaking it. It's driving me crazy."

The bartender brought Jeffrey the bill. Georgia reached inside her purse and took out cash.

"It's fine," Jeffrey said. "I invited you."

"To apologize?"

"Yes, goddamn it. To apologize."

"You invited me out to Sugar Land to apologize. A thirty-minute drive. When we both live in Montrose."

Jeffrey signed the bill.

Georgia again placed her hand on his leg.

"Fuck off," he said.

"You need to calm down and recognize—"

Jeffrey punched Georgia in the face.

"I know there are other versions," Grace said. "But that's the version Jeffrey told me. And I believe him."

Ford added a new log to the fire. It was well past midnight.

"I do worry about him," she continued. "If I were to leave him, everyone back home would take it as confirmation." She shook her head. "And the thing is there is no confirmation. Nobody knows. They talk all they want but they don't know. But that's all it takes. All someone has to do is claim something, anything, and it becomes the truth."

Ford adjusted the log before rejoining her.

"And maybe it is," she said. "I don't know. And I don't care. Except that I do care. Because if it is true." She paused to gather her thoughts. "Well, Georgia was my friend too. So if it is true, it'd hurt that much more."

# CHAPTER 10

November was nearly over. Strong winds carried crisp leaves over the asphalt, reminding Ford of anxious crabs scurrying across the streets of his childhood. He began leaving the studio earlier each day to catch a little sunlight before meeting Grace for dinner.

"Have we already run out of new places?" she teased, when he brought her back to the Grove Park Inn.

"This *is* our place," he said. "Besides, we only had drinks that first night."

They ate at the Edison Room, one of the hotel's many restaurants. Unadorned light bulbs hung above every table. Ford had reserved a window seat overlooking the mountains.

"There was a period where I tried learning the names of all the peaks," he told her.

"How many did you get?"

"Not many," he said, regretting the subject.

Learning the names had been a mistake. Names made it impossible to view the ridges behind half-closed eyes, blurring reality into fantasy, turning mountains into waves. Because waves didn't have names. Not in the way mountains did. And so Ford quit learning names.

The server arrived with Grace's Chianti and Ford's IPA. They ordered a plate of pimento cheese and barbecue pork rinds.

"You wouldn't stop staring at me," she said, reminiscing on their first encounter.

He nodded, sipping his beer. "Some people are easy to get lost in."

They had been talking this way all week.

"Even at night the view is outstanding," Grace said, looking out the window.

"It's why I moved here," Ford said. "This was the first place I came to. And this was the first view I saw. It was instantaneous."

Grace studied his face.

"What?" he asked.

"You look sad."

He shook his head. "I'm not," he assured her, returning his attention to the mountains.

In truth, he didn't often miss the ocean. Not like he used to. And back when he did, it was the idea of the ocean he missed more than anything else. The waves had lost their appeal after Bailey moved west. Ford would sometimes sit on his board for hours, legs dangling in the water, watching the action around him without the energy or interest to catch one.

"See that flashing tower?" Ford asked Grace, pointing at the mountains. "That's Mount Pisgah. To the right is Sugar Top."

She smiled. "See, you still remember."

"We ought to go hiking in the spring," he said.

Grace sipped her wine. "Look at that," she said disapprovingly. An older couple sat a few tables over. They were both staring at their phones. "Is that what it always comes to?" she asked.

"It's not so bad," Ford said. "For all you know they could be liking each other's photos of the food they're still eating."

She rolled her eyes and took another sip of wine.

Ford watched the distracted couple a moment longer. "For whatever reason, Bailey lets me follow him on Facebook," he said. "I just assume it's a fake account he created just for me."

Grace crossed her arms dramatically. "You've yet to send me a friend request," she said.

"I couldn't find you."

She grinned. Ford laughed at being caught.

"Stalker," she teased.

"How is it that you're the only person I know who *isn't* on Facebook?" he asked.

She held both hands up and out, her head tilted to the side in a state of exaggerated confusion. "Maybe I am and you're just not looking hard enough."

The server cleared their appetizer plates and inquired about additional items. Grace ordered the shrimp and grits. Ford settled on the fish and chips.

"What's your middle name," she asked Ford, once the server left.

"Willington," he said. "It's my mother's maiden name."

"Ford Willington Carson," she said. "That's a hell of a name."

"Yours?"

"Grace," she said.

"Grace Grace?" he said. "I like it."

"Evelyn Grace," she corrected him. "For whatever reason, Dr. Hudson preferred my middle name."

"I could maybe see you as an Evelyn."

"That's who I am."

They sipped their drinks, maintaining eye contact throughout.

"The night we met," she said. "Were you just hoping to get laid?"

Ford guffawed, turning a few heads. He wiped his mouth with his napkin as if to clean up the noise that had spilled out of him. "Where'd that come from?" he asked.

"Backlog," she said, deadpan.

He returned the napkin to his lap. "No," he said, matching her tone. "I wasn't looking to get laid. I was looking to be alone. But then I saw this strange, beautiful woman get socked in the head by a suicidal bird."

They both laughed out loud. The other diners again looked their way. But neither could stop.

"I mean shit," Ford said between tears. "I killed that thing for you and I still didn't get laid."

Grace wiped her eyes dry. "I'll make it up to you tonight," she said. She looked out the window. "How old are those mountains?"

Ford was thrown by how quickly her amusement abated. "Old," he said, regaining his composure. He thought about the bird again. Only now it wasn't funny. He'd never killed anything prior to that. Except cockroaches and fish.

"Do you ever miss the ocean?" she asked.

He considered her profile. Her thousand-yard stare. He knew what she was asking and he didn't want to lie. "You're always gonna miss something," he said.

She faced him. "You seemed very sad that night," she told him. "On your birthday."

"I could have been," he acknowledged.

The server approached to see about more drinks. They ordered a second round. Neither spoke for several minutes, taking back in the mountains.

"How do you want me tonight?" Grace asked. She extended her leg beneath the table, placing her foot in his lap. She had never been so overt.

"People can see," he said, looking around the dining room.

"Nobody sees anything," she said. "They're all on their phones."

The server returned with their drinks. Grace kept her foot in Ford's lap, gently massaging him. Ford smiled dumbly at the man who informed them that their food would be out shortly.

"That's excellent," Ford told him.

Grace cackled. The server maintained a tight grin.

"We're drunk," Ford told the man, hoping it'd send him on his way.

Grace bit down on her finger to control her laughter. Her toes curled around him.

"But not like *drunk* drunk," Ford assured him. "We'll behave, if that's what you're worried about. I shouldn't have said anything. We're just excited to be here."

"Very excited," Grace added. "Incredibly excited."

The server left without a word.

Grace removed her foot and whispered across the table. "I'm going to the bathroom. When you're able to, come join me."

Ford nodded.

"And when you come, I want you to say my name," she said.

He nodded again.

"Evelyn," she instructed. "Not Grace."

Ford sat alone for several minutes, counting the flashing lights on Mount Pisgah.

He found a rhythm with Grace's painting. He started with the ocean and the gray skies before tackling the chessboard. He decided to paint the centerpiece after realizing no found image would do. They were all too clean. He needed something battered and slightly warped.

The gallery's door jingled. Lenny greeted the guest. Ford remained in his studio, creating the painting's perfectly damaged focal point. Grace appeared in the doorway. Ford nearly knocked the canvas off the easel, turning it to conceal the work.

"Is that mine?" she asked.

He led her to the front of the shop. Lenny tapped the keyboard with stiff index fingers, absorbed by virtual demands. Ford didn't know where to take her. It was too cold for a walk and he'd already eaten lunch. But he didn't want her in the studio. Not then. He had found his flow and wanted to get back to it.

She apologized for interrupting. He insisted it was fine. They made small talk. He knew she sensed it. His impatience. When she apologized a second time he paused before responding, worried he might snap.

"It's fine," he said. "I just wasn't expecting you. I wanted it to be a surprise."

"I didn't see it," she promised.

"I'll see you at dinner."

She kissed him on his cheek. "I can meet you back here."

"I've got to go home first to shower."

The studio struggled to retain heat, but he had broken into a sweat during his latest session.

"I can meet you at your place," she said.

"We'll figure something out."

She apologized again before leaving.

Lenny looked up from his laptop once she was gone. "Roses are red, violets are blue, brother."

They'd planned to meet downtown at Rhu the Day. But by the time he got out of the shower, she was pulling up his driveway. He let her in before she could knock. The frigid air stung his still damp skin. She kissed him. Her cold lips matched her icicle hands. She giggled as he squirmed, until he carried her to the couch. They stayed in that evening.

The following week unfolded in a similar fashion. He spent his days searching for images to fit the fine ruins of his acrylic-based chessboard; he spent his evenings with her. Sometimes they made it out the door, but their meals were always rushed. She was ravenous and full of surprises: in the parking garage; on the second floor of the used bookstore; in the antique mall's far corner booth; on the drive back to his place.

Ford knew it couldn't last. Not at this rate. Each subsequent encounter felt more desperate and distant. Her words turned foul, her requests off-putting and strange. Ford tried attributing it to age. There was a decade between them. Every generation had its own proclivities. Perhaps this was how women born in the '80s fucked. The thought made him feel old. Shouldn't this have been his dream? Except it wasn't. Because it didn't sound real the way she said things. It sounded scripted.

He completed her collage on the final day of November. He signed and dated the back frame and brought the piece home with him that night to surprise her. Instead, she surprised him by not showing up. He didn't hear from her the next day. But as he pulled up his driveway that night he spotted her curled up on his front porch.

"What are you doing?" he asked, stepping out of his car.

She clenched her coat, shivering.

He quickened his pace. "Are you okay?"

"I didn't mean to stand you up," she said, leaning into him for warmth. "I just needed to know."

"You're freezing," he said, unlocking the door.

"I don't know what I'm doing," she said. "I have no idea what I'm doing."

"You're fine," he assured her. "Everything's okay."

She stepped back, staring at him for a moment like he was a stranger. Her fists followed, pounding into his chest. "What do you know?" she demanded. "What the fuck do you know?"

She continued to hit him. But her anger softened. Her words blurred with panic. All the while, Ford stood there shocked by the incipient sting of an unsettling revelation: He was madly in love with Evelyn Grace Burnett.

# CHAPTER 11

They both sat at their separate locations: Grace at the bar, blonde wig on, back to the crowd; Ford at his regular table, half-hoping Noire would show up. He wasn't sure why he kept coming back to Eden's. But upon spotting Grace, he wondered if she was the reason. She sat there like a statue. He didn't approach her. Nor did he stick around for a second drink.

At home his thoughts unraveled. Had she gone there knowing he'd show up? Had she been there looking for him? And had she found him? Had she spotted him at his table? Had she expected him to approach her? Was this a game?

He considered texting her but fixed a drink instead.

On his laptop, videos of Dania Beach flashed across the screen. Ford had found the footage earlier that day. In them Baily ran from crashing waves and pointed at seagulls and laughed at a lone pelican and picked up a dead crab and threw sand at Emily and paddled out with Ford.

He dozed off to the sounds of his son's former speech impediment, back when the Carsons were still the Carsons.

*The waves are cwaashing, daddy! They're cwaashing!*

*They are.*

*Why are they cwaashing, daddy?*

*They just do.*

*Where do they go after they cwaash?*

154

*They go back into the ocean and become new waves.*
*But do they always have to cwaash?*
*They wouldn't be waves if they didn't.*

At the studio the next morning, he tried focusing on the *The Suburbs*. Bailey would arrive in less than a week. But Ford's thoughts kept returning to Grace. He still had her collage. For some reason the fact eased his worries. As if the collage alone would keep her around. He hated how small he'd already become. But this was how he loved. And he knew he would take it. And he knew as he took it he'd continue to assign a deeper meaning to its bleakness.

Ford retreated to other projects. Distraction after distraction. A marathon of meaningless, brief dives into works of no consequence. Canvases that would be shipped out to parts of the country he'd never visit. To people he'd never meet. Hung on walls he'd never see.

All the while, Bailey's canvas remained blank except for those two words: *The Suburbs*.

He texted Emily: *Does our son even still like Arcade Fire?*

She answered: *If you think your son talks to me about music (or anything for that matter) you're in for a surprise.*

Ford replied: *Is that why you're sending him my way?*

She wrote: *This was his decision. I had nothing to do with it.*

Ford replied: *Well then I suppose I should be honored.*

She didn't initially answer. An hour later she forwarded him Bailey's flight information. She had emailed this to Ford the previous day. He had forgotten to respond.

He wrote: *Is he still allergic to shellfish? Cause I've got 18 candles and a crab cake waiting.*

She sent him the flight information again, followed seconds later by a winking emoji. She'd never sent him an emoji. As he looked back over the exchange, she sent him another. It read: *Lest you forget* ☺

Was she being flirtatious? He imagined her drinking a glass of white wine, flipping through the latest issue of *The New Yorker*. He sent her back a winking emoji. An odd rush followed. The thought of Shark Man stumbling upon the conversation and seeing all the emojis and wondering why in the hell his wife was sending her ex-husband anything of the sort was thrilling. The thought of Shark Man wondering evermore just what the fuck her asshole of an ex-husband was doing sending them back was equally as fun.

Ford waited, intent to answer any additional text with more yellow faces. Emily must have sensed his anticipation. She never replied.


He returned to Eden's that evening. Only this time he arrived expecting to find her there. Grace did not disappoint. She sat at the bar: same spot, same position, same wig.

When a man stepped out from behind the curtain near the side of the stage, Ford discovered Grace was using the bar's mirrored wall as a way to survey the room. She lowered her eyes as the man approached. The man scanned the area, looking at the tables, the people, and then the dancer on stage. When he stepped up to the bar, Grace placed her hand across the side of her face.

The man ordered a shot, threw it back, and glared into the crowd. Ford followed his eyes. JR stood in the middle of the room, talking to a topless dancer. He nodded compulsively, handing her money. Ford turned to Grace, who monitored JR through the mirror, watching his exchange and eventual exit. She then approached the same stripper, who offered a weary smile. The two disappeared behind the curtain near the side of the stage.

Ford left Eden's without confronting her, certain only that he had no idea what was going on.

*The waves are cwaashing, daddy! They're cwaashing!*

It was midnight and Bailey's six-year-old version observed the same things he had the previous night on Ford's laptop.

*They are.*

*Why are they cwaashing, daddy?*

Fists pounded against his front door. Ford nearly dropped his computer. The doorknob turned back and forth. The pounding continued.

*They just do.*

*Where do they go after they cwaash?*

Pound, pound, pound. Turn, turn, turn.

Ford eased the laptop onto the coffee table. His heart in his throat.

*They go back into the ocean and become new waves.*

*But do they always have to cwaash?*

157

*They wouldn't be waves if they didn't.*

"Who is it?" he yelled.

"Ford, please! Let me in," Grace shouted.

He hurried to the door. The cold night air appeared to push her through. When he closed the door, cutting off the wind, she too seemed grounded and undisturbed. The lifeless calm, which replaced her furious entry, unsettled Ford. He maintained his distance. She sat on the couch and silently watched the remaining bit of footage on his laptop.

"What are you doing?"

"Is this Bailey?" she asked, staring at the screen.

"What are you doing?" he repeated.

"I'd like to meet him," she said. "Can I?" she asked, looking Ford's way.

"What are you doing?" he demanded a third time.

"It's not as if this has been easy for me," she said.

"I haven't seen you for days and this is how you come back? You scared the shit out of me."

"I thought I heard a bear."

"Where have you been?"

He wanted to hear it. He wanted a confession. It was the only way.

Her attention returned to the computer screen.

"Where the hell have you been?"

"Don't talk like that," she said, still watching the footage.

He stepped toward her, closing the laptop.

She looked up at him, expressionless. "That was a very sweet video."

"That's not how this is going to work."

She blinked excessively and fashioned a tight grimace. "Then tell me Ford—please, please, please—tell me how it works."

He suddenly, violently, wanted her gone. Wanted her out of his life. He left her on the couch, sensing her eyes following him across the room. He returned with the collage.

"Take it and go," he said, placing the canvas next to her.

She marveled at the image. "It's almost like we planned this whole thing," she finally said.

"You're not making any sense."

"Something this beautiful can't be how things end," she said, still taking in the piece.

Ford knew he was being manipulated.

"Tell me everything," she insisted, pulling at his hand. "I want a complete analysis."

The wind outside rattled the loose gutter. The holly bush scraped against the window screen.

"My God," she said, still looking it over. "It's the entire album."

He studied her as she examined the piece. Her fingers clung to his pinky. Maybe he wasn't being manipulated. Maybe this was real.

Outside, the wind settled.

159

"It's *The Waste Land*," he said. "That's what that album is."

"*Shantih, shantih, shantih*," Grace answered, reciting the poem's final line.

Her response deflated him. This entire time he thought he'd be delivering a revelation. Of course the daughter of Dr. Hudson would have long ago made the connection.

"You and my ex-wife," he said.

"What about us?" she asked.

He hadn't meant to speak the words aloud. "You're both Eliot fans," he said. "I'd never read the poem until now."

"It's devastating," she said, still focused on the collage.

He wasn't sure if she meant the poem or his interpretation of it. The good works always made him arrogant, even though he knew his images never would have existed without their guidance. But he also understood that his renditions extended original works, creating a new ripple. That's what he loved about the process—how a poem written in 1922 and first published in London could inspire a five-track album composed in 2011 by an indie rock band based in Houston could lead to a visual rendering in 2015 by a lone man in Asheville. There was something beautiful and deathless about it. Ford thought of Phlebas, the drowned Phoenician sailor, whose bones now scattered across the canvas, which Grace still surveyed inside a warm home on the side of a cold, ancient mountain.

"I love it," she said. "I absolutely love it." She kissed him. He didn't resist. When they parted, her eyes widened. "Have you finished Bailey's?" she asked. "I want to see it."

The question scattered his thoughts. He wanted to be back in that previous moment, back in the ephemeral bliss of briefly sensing time's endlessness. He tried remembering the lines about Phlebas—the stages of his age and youth entering the whirlpool. He spotted the pair of pearls floating in the ocean. Those were his eyes. But Ford couldn't see the rest of it anymore.

"I spoke with his mother the other day," Ford said. "He doesn't really listen to Arcade Fire anymore. So I've tabled it."

Grace didn't respond.

"Plus, it'd be a hassle to fly back with a canvas that size. I hadn't thought about that until his mother brought it up," Ford said, continuing the lie. "And at his age they just want money more than anything."

Grace smiled at him with sad eyes. "Can I meet him?"

Ford stepped back. "What are we doing?" he asked.

She considered the question. "I've been trying to figure out my husband," she said.

"You still love him."

"A little bit," she said. "I don't want to. But I do."

His desire was immediate. Not for sex. He wanted Grace's honesty directed at him, about him. Ford needed her to tell him who he was.

"Everything's happening so fast," she said.

He didn't know how to convey his need. He looked briefly back over Phlebas' lost pearls.

"Do you not want this?" she asked.

"I do," he said.

"Then let's not worry."

"How could we not?"

"Do you love me?" she asked.

"You keep disappearing."

"But do you love me?"

"My answer won't change any of that."

She kissed him again and he kissed back. Her lips left his, finding their way down his neck. As she unbuttoned him, he returned to her collage, studying the fine pile of dust stacked on the middle of the chessboard. He thought about Bailey's blank canvas. He thought about Grace in the blonde wig at Eden's. He thought about JR stepping out of the club. He thought about Emily's emojis. He thought about Eliot's words: *I Tiresias, old man with wrinkled dugs / Perceived the scene, and foretold the rest— / I too awaited the expected guest.*

Grace led Ford to the couch, seating him next to the collage. She had undressed them both. He stared at Jane Fellow's encaustic painting above the mantle as Grace eased him inside of her.

He thought about their first meeting. He thought about Virginia and Bob Smith. He thought about Florida and the ocean—a lone pelican, a dead crab, crashing waves.

Grace guided his mouth onto her left nipple. He thought about Emily's recollection of sand easing between her fingers those many years ago. He still couldn't place it. But it was there. Grace pressed her hand against the back of his head, encouraging him. He pinched her with his teeth and

162

everything melted. Except for Eliot's words: *One must be so careful these days.*

# CHAPTER 12

Years before Bailey and his mother moved west, Ford took his son to Los Angeles. The trip had been a surprise gift for Bailey's twelfth birthday. Winter always made for the best rides. Everyone assumed the opposite, but it wasn't true. If you wanted the big ones you had to suffer. And for a week straight they suffered, catching giant wave after giant wave.

On their final day a local shop owner told them about Zeroes, a quiet little spot at the northern edge of Los Angeles County. They rode six-footers all morning. By noon Ford was exhausted, giving in to the sand. But Bailey couldn't be stopped.

Ford watched his son's tireless pursuit and wondered what he might become. Anything could happen, Ford thought. Bailey rose with the winds and then plummeted into the ocean, climbing back onto his board and paddling toward the horizon. He could lose himself in a girl or grow weary of the surf scene. But as Bailey pushed himself to his feet, bending his knees, Ford knew this was it. He couldn't imagine his boy anywhere else but on the water. The ocean was where he belonged. It was his bliss.

And then it happened. Bailey entered a tube. Ford shot up from the sand and ran parallel to the wave. In all his years surfing he'd never experienced a tube. Everything around him went quiet as he followed his son's blurry form inside the hollow. And then it was over. Bailey jetted out just before the wave crashed and immediately ran ashore, throwing his board on the sand.

They both initially laughed because neither could speak. Overwhelmed by the experience, Bailey soon cried. Embarrassed, he looked back at the ocean until he found the right words. "Holy shit!" he said.

Ford smiled.

Bailey hugged his father. His cold wetsuit pressed into Ford's warm skin. Ford stared out onto the water, his chin resting against his son's soaked hair. "Holy shit," Ford agreed.

In the days leading up to Bailey's arrival, Ford and Grace reversed roles. He was now avoiding her. But whereas Grace would have withdrawn completely, Ford never cut ties. Nor did he intend to. They texted daily.

*I can't sleep at night,* he wrote her.

*You're excited,* she replied.

He wanted it to be that. But it wasn't. Bailey's arrival felt like meeting a new client. There would be so much to navigate. So much to interpret. So much to second-guess.

*I haven't seen him in years,* Ford texted her.

*This'll change all that,* she wrote back.

*Or it might just remind him why he kept his distance in the first place,* Ford replied.

Grace's response arrived in three scrambled texts: the second came first, the first came second and the third stayed in place.

Once unscrambled, it read:

*I think it's so brave what you're doing. And I say that with complete knowledge that this might turn out different than what you expect. (I don't really know what you expect.) I'm not trying to be cynical either. That's just the truth. That's why I think it's so brave. And wonderful. It's much easier to just let things go until all parties act as if it never even happened. Or worse, pretend it isn't broken and just leave it at that.*

She called him.

"Did I upset you?" she asked.

"No," he said, thrown by the question. But he quickly understood. He hadn't responded. He'd been too busy figuring out the sequence of her texts. He apologized, explaining to her what happened.

"That's weird," she said.

"I'm glad you called," he told her. "I missed your voice."

"You're sweet."

"I've been moody," he said, feeling a sudden urge to explain himself.

"I didn't mean to upset you," she said.

"You didn't."

"But if I did."

"You didn't," he repeated.

The conversation was starting to play on his nerves. His neck ran hot, his fingers cold. He wanted to tell her something terrible about himself. So that there would be no surprises. Not that she didn't already know. An absent father can't hide his absenteeism. How could he resent her for giving him the benefit of the doubt? The very thought nearly broke him.

"It's going to be great," she said.

He didn't know what to say. He looked at his watch. Bailey would land in less than nine hours. A spark flew out of his fireplace. He stepped on the dying ember with his bare foot.

"I'll let you know when he gets in," Ford said. "The three of us can grab dinner."

"Okay," she said.

He couldn't gauge her response. Had her tone shifted? Was she disappointed by the suggestion? Was that not what she wanted?

"You should get some rest," she said.

He turned his back to the fire, peering out the window toward his neighbor's place. The television was off.

"Okay," he said, doing his best to mimic her ambiguous tone.


Bailey was more handsome than what his Facebook pictures revealed. His skin glowed a deep caramel. His brown wavy hair gathered behind his ears. But his true appeal stemmed from his walk: he kept his eyes straight ahead while his chin tilted slightly upward. Even if Bailey hadn't been Ford's son, Ford would have admired the certainty of Bailey's strut. The fact that this boy was his son made it that much better. He and

Emily had had an ugly marriage, but no one could argue that they hadn't created something beautiful.

Bailey passed the security checkpoint. To Ford's relief his son smiled at him. He didn't know what to say.

"This airport's tiny," Bailey offered as an icebreaker. His voice was deep. Deeper than what he sounded like over the phone.

"How was the flight?"

Bailey shrugged.

"You got luggage?" Ford asked, pointing toward the carousel.

Bailey tugged on the strap of his backpack.

Ford patted the shoulder of his son's denim jean jacket. "That's not very thick," he said.

Bailey wore a sweater underneath. He pulled its hood over his head. "You sound like Mom," he said.

Ford hesitated. "Well, it's fucking cold out there."

Bailey grinned. "See, now you're trying too hard."

Ford looked around the airport, imagining a limousine driver standing somewhere with a sign that read, *Mr. Carson: Run!*

"You look like the Unabomber with that thing on," he told Bailey.

"Unibrow?"

"Unabomber," Ford repeated.

"What does that mean?"

"Ted Kaczynski."

Bailey twisted his lips.

"Forget it," Ford said.

Bailey received two phone calls on the drive out. One was from his agent. Ford knew this because twice his son said, "Rick, you're my fucking agent." The other call came midway through the first. It was Emily. Ford knew this because Bailey said, "Rick, I've got take this . . . Because it's my fucking mother." Unlike with his agent, Bailey turned away from Ford while speaking to Emily in a series of mumbled yeses and noes.

Ford didn't want to eavesdrop, despite his emerging paranoia. What might she be asking him? *Does he look drunk? Does he smell drunk? Does he talk drunk?* Ford grinned at the passing cars. Anything to divert his attention.

The conversation dragged on. Five minutes in, Ford resented Emily for calling. A check-in would have been fine. But this was excessive. Did she plan to keep this up for the next five days? There was a long pause on Bailey's end, followed by another series of mumbled yeses and noes. What the fuck was she asking him?

Bailey was silent after the call. Ford didn't pry. He knew better. Bailey would report back everything to Emily. He always had. So Ford brought up lunch. His son continued to stare straight ahead, arms crossed. Bailey said he'd eaten before his connection in Atlanta. Ford tried making small talk. Bailey didn't play along.

"I've been watching old footage," Ford continued, undeterred by his son's indifference. "Remember Zeroes?"

Bailey's head turned swiftly. "You got that shit on tape?"

"No," Ford said. "Most of the footage is from Dania. It just reminded me of the trip. That was a good time."

Bailey exhaled. "That sucks."

"What sucks?"

"I thought you filmed it maybe. That'd've been dope as shit. My first tube. Fuck. That'd've gotten me like 50,000 likes."

"But you remember it?" Ford asked.

"Hell yeah," Bailey said.

A white Odyssey blocked their exit at the off-ramp. Its hazards flashed. A woman stood in front of the van, visible only from the shoulders up.

"What the fuck is she doing?" Bailey asked.

A car pulled up behind them and honked. Bailey spun around in his seat, glaring at the driver.

The woman stepped toward the rear of the van. She was pregnant. Shuffling through the back seat, she emerged with a plastic grocery bag. The car behind Ford laid on its horn a second time. The woman causing the traffic jam didn't react. She disappeared around the front of the van, reappearing with a bloody possum. She used the plastic bag as a barrier between herself and the creature, placing the animal on the side of the road.

"Oh, what the fuck?" Bailey said.

The driver behind Ford yelled out his window, unaware of all that transpired before them. Bailey reached for the door. Ford grabbed him by the sleeve of his jacket.

"That guy needs to shut the fuck up," Bailey said.

The possum stood on unstable legs. The woman covered her mouth and stared as blood leaked from the creature's ears and nose. The driver behind them honked a third time.

Bailey rushed out of the car before Ford could stop him. Instead of confronting the incensed driver, Bailey approached the woman. She didn't initially respond. But soon the two were conversing. Bailey led her back to the van, helping her inside. She rolled down the window and placed her hand on his wrist, patting it gently. The two exchanged a few more words and then the woman drove off.

Bailey retrieved the bloody bag.

Ford rolled down his window. "What are you doing?"

His son used the bag to pick up the possum. He placed the animal back on the road.

"What are you doing?" Ford repeated.

Bailey approached the window. Blood stained the sleeves of his jacket.

"That thing could have rabies," Ford said.

Bailey leaned into the car. "You got to take care of it."

The driver behind them demanded that they move. Bailey left his father and placed the bloody bag beneath the driver's windshield wiper. The man cried out.

Bailey rejoined his father inside the car. He pointed at the possum. "It's suffering," he said. "You've got to help it out."

Ford thought about the bird at the Grove Park Inn. He eased off the brake. The front tire lifted slightly. Behind them the man turned on his windshield wipers, hoping perhaps the bag would come loose. Instead, it spread the blood. Ford's back tire rose then fell. He didn't look back.

Lenny pulled Bailey in for a hug as if the two knew each other. To Ford's surprise, Bailey embraced Lenny. Lenny kept repeating the fact that Bailey looked too tan for these parts. Bailey told Lenny about the possum. Lenny shook his head throughout.

"Got me a cousin over in Black Mountain," Lenny told Bailey. "Black Mountain's just east of us here. An EMT driver, my cousin. Had him a call a few years back, near midnight. Dark as all can be out there. And so he's driving up Old Nine when—bam!" Lenny slapped together his hands. "Took out an entire family of bears. Mother and two cubs. And see my cousin he's seen things. Was over in Iraq. But them bears affected him. Which is to say, you can't never tell what's gonna do it to you till it does."

Bailey nodded dumbly. Lenny burst with laughter and pulled him in, pretending to give Bailey a noogie. He then toured the boy around the space.

Alone inside his studio, Ford watched gray clouds roll in from the west. They looked pregnant with snow. He imagined a blizzard. He then imagined Bailey in his denim, bloodstained jacket, chattering a painful grin. Ford suddenly felt his tire lift over the possum. He shuffled through day old mail, tossing out multiple life insurance offers from AAA. He texted Grace about Bailey's arrival. They agreed to meet at Myrtle's Twenty-One for dinner. Lenny and Bailey appeared in the doorway.

"Had I known we had us a surf legend visiting, I'd've of bought me a board for him to sign," Lenny told Ford.

"You knew that he surfs."

"Yeah, but you ain't told me just all *where* he's surfed. This boy here's Carmen Sandiego."

"No, I live in L.A.," Bailey said, not catching the reference.

"Looks like it might snow," Ford said, pointing toward the window.

"Tell me the name of the video again," Lenny asked Bailey.

"Just YouTube my name."

"It's B-A-I-L-E-Y Carson?"

"Just YouTube Wolf Storms, Nicaragua," Bailey said.

"Shoot," Lenny said. "Write me that down on a piece of a paper. I'm no good when it comes to that sort of thing."

The front door opened. Lenny left them to greet the visitor. "Long time no see," he called out.

Bailey lingered in his father's studio, unaware that his unfinished birthday gift leaned against the easel. *The Suburbs* since painted over.

Ford hurried to the front, hopeful for another surprise visit from Grace. Instead, the mailman waved to Ford on his way out.

"I'm hungry," Bailey said.

Ford's attention remained on the empty doorway. What if he just walked out? Lenny would be a good host. He'd show

173

Bailey around. The two of them would probably have a far better time together than he and Bailey ever would.

Bailey repeated himself.

Ford turned to his son. "I asked in the car if you wanted lunch."

"I wasn't hungry in the car."

"Tell me the name of that video again," Lenny called from behind the counter.

But Bailey was already out the door.

"We probably won't be back," Ford said.

Lenny nodded, a bit solemn. "I'll hold down the fort, brother."


Bailey pretended to sleep in the passenger seat on their way home from lunch. Ford did the math in his head. Something like one hundred more hours. He hoped a rhythm would develop. He reminded himself that Bailey probably was just tired. He had flown cross-country. Ford looked at his son who continued to feign sleep. The car rattled across the train tracks, forcing Bailey's hand.

"Place reminds me of Cristobal," Bailey said, taking in the scenery. "Just no ocean."

Ford knew about Hawaii. And he'd talked with Bailey before his son went to Australia a few years back. But he'd never heard about Cristobal. He pretended otherwise before changing the subject.

"I've got a friend joining us for dinner tonight," he said.

But Bailey wasn't listening. He kept talking about Cristobal.

They drove past the Methodist church at the base of the mountain. Bailey read its signboard aloud. "*Don't wait for the hearse to take you to church.*" He laughed. "I didn't know religious people had a sense of humor."

They pulled into Ford's driveway.

"Shit man," Bailey said, stepping out of the car. "This here's the real deal. Look at that fucking view."

Ford faced the mountains, nodding as if he'd been unaware of his surroundings until his son pointed it out.

"If this place had a beach it'd be tits," Bailey said.

"It'd be what?"

But Bailey was already up the slope, approaching the front door.

"It might be unlocked," Ford called out. "My girlfriend tends to forget."

Bailey grinned. "You got a lady, huh?"

Ford didn't know why he introduced Grace this way. She didn't even have a key. "Sometimes," he said, approaching the door. "You'll meet her at dinner."

"She a babe?"

Ford ignored the question. He opened the door and headed for the kitchen, pulling out a bottle of whiskey. Bailey's eyes glowed as Ford poured them each a celebratory shot. They touched glasses. Bailey winced. Embarrassed, he started talking about a few of his buddies based out of Hawaii and what all they drank—Tornado Todd and Sunset Sammy and a handful of others with alliterative nicknames.

"We'll have another one when you turn nineteen," Ford said, twisting on the cap.

Bailey rolled his eyes before turning on his heels to inspect the place. He approached the mantle, looking over Jane Fellow's encaustic painting. "This yours?"

"A friend of mine did it," Ford said, joining his son.

Bailey leaned in nearly touching the canvas with his nose. "What's it made of? Clay?"

"Wax," Ford said. "We can swing by her studio tomorrow if you want."

"It looks like a giant wave."

"She did it for this woman's son."

"Is this the same woman you're banging?"

"You need to watch your mouth."

"I'm just asking."

"You're pushing it."

"Does your lady's son live here?" Bailey asked, looking back over the wave.

"This has nothing to do with Grace."

"Who's Grace?"

"My girlfriend."

"So she doesn't have a son?"

"No," Ford said. "This painting was for a different woman. I hardly knew her."

"Why'd she give you the painting then?"

"It's a long story," Ford said. He briefly entertained the idea of telling Bailey about the lie he told Virginia Smith. To his relief the thought unsettled him. At the very least he had some decency, some fatherly instinct.

"Her son died," was all he said. "It was a commemorative piece. But she couldn't handle it."

Bailey considered the news. "I sure hope her son made it to church before the hearse ride."

Ford laughed through his nose.

Bailey refocused on the piece. "It looks like a wave on acid."

Ford stared at his son with harsh, cold eyes.

Bailey grinned. "Oh, right," he said. "Forgot you're not supposed to say those kinds of things in front of your dad."

They arrived downtown at a quarter past eight. Bailey had again feigned sleep during the ride out. Grace texted Ford as they emerged from the parking garage, letting him know she'd grabbed them a table in the back.

A three-piece jazz band played near the hostess stand. Bailey eyed the bar. When the song ended the diners clapped.

"Where's your lady?" he asked.

"I can't have you running your mouth tonight," Ford said.

"I didn't say anything."

"Her name is Grace," he said. "Not my *lady*. Not my *babe*. Not my *tits*."

"Your *tits*?"

"Listen," he said, "I'm trying, okay?"

"Trying to make yourself look good."

"I'm trying to let you know," he said. "That's all."

The band started into its next song.

"I'm not gonna cock-block you," Bailey shouted into Ford's ear.

Ford didn't respond.

Bailey laughed. "I'm kidding," he said. "I'll be good, I swear. Listen, I'm hungry and this band sucks. Can we find your lady—I mean Grace. Can we find your Grace and fucking eat already."

"Watch your mouth."

"Fuck, shit, cunt, cock," he said. "There. It's all out of me."


Grace stood to greet them. Bailey offered an awkward hand. She hesitated before accepting. He barely made eye contact. She smiled at Ford, uncertain. Ford grimaced. The three sat.

Grace handled the early conversation. She gave Bailey an overview of his own biography to let him know she'd heard plenty about him. Bailey remained practically mute, nodding most of his responses.

When the server arrived, Bailey was quick to order, presenting a fake ID. The server looked it over and briefly glanced Ford's way before eyeing Grace. Ford tried to imagine what the server thought. Grace looked young enough to be either of their dates. The server handed Bailey back the card. Ford pointed to Grace, inviting her to order. She held her glass to show she'd already been served.

"Water?" Ford asked.

She nodded.

"He'll have the same," Bailey said, ordering for Ford.

The server disappeared around the corner.

"That card's mine when we get back to the house," Ford told Bailey.

"'Cause you never had one."

"I didn't flaunt it in front of my father."

"But you had one," Bailey insisted.

Ford leaned back in his chair.

"How do like Asheville?" Grace asked Bailey.

"It reminds me of Cristobal," he said. "Minus the ocean."

"I've never been," she said.

"It looks a lot like this but with an ocean."

"That's so interesting," she said, eyes desperately wide.

A loud crash sounded near the bar. Their server hovered over a series of broken plates and glasses. Bailey laughed out loud.

"They've got ribs here," Ford said, pointing at his son's menu.

Bailey didn't respond.

"Ribs," Ford repeated.

"Is that like their specialty or something?" Bailey asked.

"You love ribs."

"Since when?"

"I drove all over Lancaster, Pennsylvania trying to find ribs for this guy," Ford told Grace, reliving the whole scene. "At your great-uncle Chuck's funeral," he reminded Bailey. He turned back to Grace. "He loves ribs."

"The lamb looks tight," Bailey said.

Ford glared at his son, who continued to read over the menu. When Ford turned to Grace, he realized she'd been staring at him glaring at Bailey. They exchanged hesitant smiles.

"Speaking of lambs, I had a dream last night that I was on a hill with a whole herd of them," Grace told Ford. "Or maybe they were sheep. I confuse the two. But I was on the hill and you were on another hill and we had cans but no wire connecting them. But we could still hear each other. And I kept telling you about the lambs and you kept insisting they were elephants."

The server returned with their beers. Ford asked about getting Grace a cocktail, but she insisted she was fine. She ordered appetizers for the table. Afterward, the three toasted.

"But this is it for you," Ford told Bailey, eyeing his son's beer.

"That's fine," Bailey said. "As long as we can have more of that whiskey later," he said, winking.

Their glasses briefly touched.

"You kept telling me it was going to snow," Grace said, returning to her dream. She put her hand over Ford's wrist. "You said the elephants were going to be covered in snow. And I kept insisting they were lambs. But they might have been sheep."

Ford didn't bother telling her that lambs were baby sheep.

"I had a dream a few months back where my buddy Toro was grinding my wisdom teeth down and packing them in a bowl for us to smoke," Bailey said. "Which is weird because when I woke up my mouth hurt, but I didn't even have my wisdom teeth yet. But then like last week one of the bottom ones showed up. None of the others, though."

"Wisdom teeth are the worst," Grace said. "I had mine taken out in college. I couldn't eat or talk for a week."

"How old are you?" Bailey asked.

"Hey," Ford said sharply.

"Twenty-nine," Grace answered. "What about you Ford?"

She had already mastered the role of the peacekeeping mother.

"Forty," he said.

She laughed, but he could hear the effort. "Not your age. I was talking about dreams."

"I don't dream."

"God you're boring," Bailey said.

"Everyone dreams," Grace insisted, smiling stiffly.

"I never remember mine," Ford said.

181

Bailey brought back up his travels: Nicaragua, Canary Islands, Riyue Bay, Iquique.

Ford had never even heard of some of these places. He excused himself and headed for the restroom. He took his time at the urinal, exhausted by his son.

Bailey was still talking when Ford rejoined the table.

"My other buddy Buddha," Bailey told Grace, "fucking legendary. Dude's gonna be the next Kelly Slater. He's like that fucking good, right? But he also happens to be a genius. I mean he totally transcends the sport. Makes it more than just a sport. Makes it an art form. I mean he's doing things people haven't done. He's straight walking water. Got this kind of religious understanding of the ocean. This complete oneness. The way he talks about it—it's like I can't even describe it. That's why we call him Buddha. Holy shit. Pure genius."

"You called me a *weirdo*," Ford practically shouted.

Both Grace and Bailey turned to him, awaiting an explanation.

"When I used to talk that way," he continued, lowering his voice. "*Nobody gives a fuck*? You don't remember? How if I *surfed them more than I talked them*, your friends wouldn't think I was such a *weirdo*. None of that rings a bell?"

Bailey's chin receded into his neck. "I never said that."

"Yes you did."

"When?"

"When we were still in Florida."

Bailey's nostrils flared. "I was like twelve."

"Well, you said it."

"Okay," Bailey said. "Sorry I said something I don't remember."

"I could use that same excuse."

"Except I was kid," Bailey reminded him. "And notice that I apologized."

"You still are a kid."

"For one more night, maybe."

"Oh, right," Ford said. "I forgot."

Bailey turned to Grace. "Anyway. We're shooting a surf video in Hawaii next month. Buddha's way more famous but he's not possessive, you know? He shares it. He's always tagging me in shit and retweeting my stuff."

The server returned with two more beers and an appetizer of fried green tomatoes.

"I got us another round," Bailey said, taking a sip.

Grace avoided looking at Ford. She smiled at the server and ordered the chicken salad. Bailey got the lamb. Ford settled on the ribs. Bailey was already halfway through his second beer by the time the server walked off.

"Where is it?" Ford asked.

"Where is what?" Grace answered, her voice unnaturally chipper.

"Your ID," he said to Bailey.

"In my wallet."

"Where'd you get it?"

"My buddy got it for me for my birthday."

"Let me see it," Ford said.

"Hell no."

The two stared each other down. They hadn't even been together for a solid twelve hours, Ford thought. How could they already be this comfortable with hating each other?

"This reduced balsamic is amazing," Grace said, pointing at the plate with her fork. "Ford, try this."

"I just want to see it," he said, ignoring Grace.

"Why?"

Grace served them both a fried tomato. "Can I see it?" she then asked Bailey.

Bailey stabbed at the tomato before handing her the ID.

She was suddenly Ford's wife, Bailey their child. But Ford was still Ford.

"You don't even look like this Devon Walker," she said, laughing as she studied the ID. She held it beside him and chuckled. "No, you're much more handsome."

Bailey lowered his eyes toward the table and focused on his tomato.

Ford grinned. "What's the matter Devon Walker?" he teased. "You shy all of a sudden?"

Bailey ignored him.

"You don't look like a Walker," Ford said, still teasing. "Certainly not a Devon."

Grace handed Bailey back the ID.

"What do I look like then?" Bailey asked.

"Like you're blushing," Ford said.

Grace gently tapped Ford under the table with her foot.

184

"Devon's my sister's name," Bailey told her. "My buddy didn't realize that before he scored the card. Not that it matters. Devon's one of those anthropological names."

"You mean *androgynous?*" Ford asked.

"You sound like Mom." Bailey slid the ID into his pocket. "She's always correcting people on their words," he told Grace.

"I do that too sometimes," Grace admitted.

Bailey sipped his beer.

"Enjoy that drink, Devon Walker," Ford said. "'Cause it's your last."

"Do you still think it's a stripper's name?" Bailey asked.

The question confused Ford.

Bailey patted a limp wrist against his chest. "The *downy* stripper?"

"What are you talking about?" Ford asked.

"My sister," he said to Grace. "He told me she was gonna have Down syndrome. He said my mom was too old to have another baby. And then when that didn't happen he told me Devon was a stripper's name."

"I never said that."

"Why would I make that shit up?"

Grace looked away, her clenched jaw holding back whatever thoughts she had.

Bailey sipped his beer before raising it for a toast. Ford kept his glass on the table. Bailey lifted his higher. Ford told him to put it down. Bailey told Ford to meet him halfway.

When Ford didn't budge, Bailey tilted his glass, threatening to spill it. Ford raised his beer and they toasted. But Bailey wasn't satisfied. He insisted they do it again.

"Eye contact," he said. "You can't toast without eye contact."

Ford obliged. Bailey nodded and then nearly finished the remainder of his drink in a single gulp. Grace slowly cut into her tomato without lifting a single slice off her plate.

"What'd you get me for my birthday?" Bailey asked.

"You'll find out tomorrow."

"But what'd you get me?"

"Don't worry about it," Ford said.

"He forgets every year," Bailey told Grace.

"I do not."

"But he means well," Bailey continued, smirking at Ford. "He makes it a point to call every so often to remind me that. That he means well. And then he'll bitch about my mom."

"*Zeroes*," Ford exclaimed. "That was for your birthday."

"Oh yeah," Bailey said. "How could I forget? That *one* time."

The table fell silent. Bailey took out his phone. Grace scanned the dining room. Ford looked in the direction of the band.

When the food arrived, Bailey chewed his lamb loudly.

"How is it?" Grace asked.

"Lamby," he said, taking another bite.

186

The two conversed throughout the meal while Ford quietly picked at the ribs. When Bailey left to use the restroom, silence ensued.

"He shouldn't have ordered that second round," Ford finally spoke.

Grace wouldn't look at him.

Ford repeated himself.

Grace peered across the table. "Are you suggesting it's my fault?" she asked. "Is that what you're getting at? That it was on me to stop him? He's not my son, Ford. You were in the bathroom."

"That's not what I was saying at all," he protested. "I'm just saying he shouldn't have had another drink. He can't control himself."

"You mean he's talking too much."

"His fake ID," Ford said, ignoring her comment. "I'd've never done that sort of thing in front of my father."

"Maybe he doesn't think of you that way."

"What the fuck's that supposed to mean?"

"What the fuck's what supposed to mean?" Bailey asked, returning to the table.

Grace smiled, picking back up their previous conversation. But Bailey didn't fall for it. He repeated the question. Grace considered a response. She settled on, "What the fuck's what supposed to mean?"

"That's what I'm asking," Bailey said, confused.

"You shouldn't have had that second beer," she told him. "You're cursing like a sailor."

"He's the one who cursed first," he said, pointing at Ford.

When Ford asked for the check, the server smiled and raised an eyebrow, extending his arm in Bailey's direction. Ford didn't understand. He repeated his request. The server again pointed at Bailey who grinned. "The gentleman took care of it," the server informed Ford.

"Should have let me buy you another round," Bailey said, wiggling his brow.

"Why would you do that?" Ford asked his son.

The server lingered.

"I suppose you saw his real name on the credit card?" Ford asked the man.

The server walked away.

Bailey stood. "I paid cash." He tossed his napkin onto the table and tucked in his chair. "I'm not a kid."

He waited for Ford to respond.

"Did you tip him?" Ford asked.

Bailey laughed. "He thinks I'm a kid," he said to Grace, holding out his hand for her.

The two walked ahead of Ford on the sidewalk. The wind rolled in from the west, cutting through alleyways and side streets. Ford followed them into the garage. Only after they reached Grace's car did he remember they'd driven separately. She was parked one floor below them.

Bailey gave her a hug. She looked over his shoulder at Ford. Ford wondered if this would be the last time he'd see her, aware that he had shown her a side she could not forget. Bailey released her.

"Happy birthday," she told him.

"It isn't till tomorrow," he reminded her.

Her eyes beamed. "We got you something," she said, searching for her keys.

Grace opened the trunk of her car and pulled out the collage. Ford realized then that he hadn't titled it. In a way it remained unfinished. Looking it over, he wasn't sure what he would have called it. His eyes locked in on the image of Lil, the only woman present on the board except for Marie. But Marie was a child, sledding down the dust. Lil was the only woman, tired and lifeless. He'd found the illustration inside an old hardback *Reader's Digest* from 1959.

"Is this one of yours?" Bailey asked Ford.

Ford turned to Grace. She nodded, encouraging him to go along with it. To put aside his hurt feelings. Suddenly she was his wife again and Bailey was their son. But Ford was still Ford.

"What song is it?" Bailey asked.

Ford was surprised that his son knew about his process. "I tried doing Arcade Fire's *The Suburbs.* Not the song but the whole album," he said. "But I couldn't get it."

"What is it then?" Bailey asked.

"I don't really know," Ford lied.

"So then like—what the fuck is it?"

Ford stared at Grace, hoping she'd save him. But he knew she wouldn't. And she didn't. She stood there watching him, waiting. He was a man thrown overboard. She had already tossed him a life vest. What else did he want from her?

He tried responding but nothing came. He told Bailey to say goodnight to Grace.

"We just did."

"Well, you didn't say thank you."

"It was all your father's doing," Grace told Bailey. "He just needed me to hold on to it so you wouldn't find it."

She was again his wife, talking at him through their son.

"Goodbye, Bailey," she said, looking at Ford. She returned her attention to Bailey. "I'm glad we were able to meet."

"I'll be here all week," he reminded her.

"That's right," she said, nodding. "It's just—well, I might not be."

# CHAPTER 13

There were no leaves to look at on the parkway, but Bailey sat alert throughout the drive. Ford was pleased that his son remained both awake and off his phone. Whenever they approached a tunnel, Bailey became a child again, sucking in as much air as he could hold before they entered darkness. Always, Ford eased off the gas, eliciting Bailey's playful punches. Once they met the other side of daylight, Bailey released a loud, dramatic exhale.

On the trail they walked in silence, enclosed by the cluttered rhododendron. Slowly and without intention, Bailey separated from Ford. Despite the low temperature, Ford began shedding layers. His legs grew tired, his breath short.

At the peak, Bailey stood atop one of the two wooden benches situated at the lookout. His hand shielded his forehead, casting a shadow over his eyes. He faced east. "This is amazing," he said.

Ford smiled, still recovering from the climb. The wind whirled through the dead limbs, washing over them. Bailey leapt from the bench, pointing out the reservoir in the valley below. With his back to Ford, he asked, "Did you move here to spite Mom?"

The question came out of nowhere.

"Is that what she told you?" Ford said, upset by how defensive he sounded.

Bailey turned around. The wind tossed his hair across his eyes. "No," he said, combing his fingers through his wild locks. "I overheard her say it once to Mima."

"What did Mima say?"

Ford knew he shouldn't have asked.

Bailey shrugged. "I don't know," he said. "They were talking on the phone."

Ford understood what his son was getting at—why Asheville and not Los Angeles? He remembered meeting Emily at the Starbucks inside the Port St. Lucy rest stop. She was six months pregnant with her and Shark Man's second and final child, the infamous Devon. Somehow on the drive up to meet her, Ford had convinced himself that Emily was going to confide in him about her plans to leave Shark Man. Instead she informed him about California.

"We're practically living there as it is with all these competitions," she said. "Plus, all the trips to Hawaii. It just makes sense."

"It always *just makes sense*," Ford said.

"You could have easily moved to Cocoa Beach."

"If that makes you feel better."

"I'm here to extend the invitation."

"I don't need your permission."

"That's not what an invitation is," Emily said.

"How is it that we've been divorced now for five years and you're still trying to get me to sell the business?"

"I'm asking you to be part of your son's life."

"Fuck you."

Emily stood and headed for the exit.

"Was he too scared to tell me himself?" Ford called after her.

She returned to the table, unwilling to share their conversation with strangers. "Are you referring to your son or to my husband?"

Her words stung. He couldn't remember her ever referring to Shark Man this way. Like she was rubbing it in his face.

"Bailey," he barked. "Bailey couldn't tell me himself?"

"No," she said. "And do you know why?"

He sipped his latte.

"Because he was terrified you wouldn't give a shit," she said.

Ford didn't know what to say. He kept sipping his latte. Emily shook her head and exited the rest stop.

"Mom told me once that you're a lot like your dad," Bailey said.

Ford studied his son, bewildered. "You remember your granddad."

Bailey shook his head.

"He used to give you airplane rides."

Bailey shrugged.

"Yeah, well, your mother's a lot like her mom," Ford said. "Mima means well, but she blamed Hugh for everything. Your poor granddad could never do anything right."

"Pop Pop hated your guts," Bailey said.

"Yeah, well, Hugh and I had our differences."

Another breeze blew over them. Bailey leapt from the bench, landing a few feet in front of Ford. "I realize you're not a complete asshole," he said. "But I get how you might be if your dad was an asshole."

"Your granddad wasn't an asshole."

"What I don't get," Bailey continued, "is how I'm such an asshole."

"You're not an asshole," Ford said, crushed by the statement.

Bailey scrutinized his father.

"You're not," Ford insisted. "You're just full of yourself. It's one of the best parts about being a teenager. You haven't yet realized how irrelevant you truly are."

Bailey didn't initially respond.

"You're not irrelevant," Ford backtracked. "That's not what I meant."

"I'm afraid of turning into you," Bailey said.

"What am I supposed to say to something like that?"

Bailey turned his back on his father. "I didn't mean to fuck things up last night."

"You didn't," Ford said, surprised by the shift in his son's tone.

"I cock-blocked you," Bailey said. "That's like the worst thing a dude can to another dude."

"I'm not a dude."

Bailey turned around. "What are you then?"

Ford took a deliberate breath. He recognized that Bailey wasn't asking it to be mean or to instigate a fight. His son was posing a genuine question.

"Apparently, I'm the asshole father you're scared of turning into," Ford answered, unsure if his response would suffice but certain it was the best he could offer.

Bailey stared at Ford. "Why'd you move here for real?" he asked.

Ford wished that he knew. Maybe it had been out of spite. Or was it pure desperation? Or some combination of the two? He'd told so many stories to so many people about his decision to move. It had been for the mountains, for the music, for the climate—none of which was true.

"I thought it was my best chance to start over," he said. "I wasn't handling things particularly well back then."

Despite the cold, a flash of heat burned Ford's skin. He couldn't look at his son, afraid of what he might see. His fear was humiliating.

"It's nice out here," Bailey said.

Ford was thrown by Bailey's response. He had expected fire. "I sometimes miss the smell of the ocean," he said.

"It's a good smell," Bailey agreed.

Ford didn't understand the calm exchange, but he wanted to keep it going.

"Do you like Los Angeles?" he asked.

"I just like the ocean," Bailey said.

Bailey folded his hair behind his ears, revealing his solemn eyes lost on the horizon.

It always shocked Ford when it happened, no matter who Bailey suddenly resembled. Sometimes he looked like Ford's father. Other times his expression matched Hugh's. In this particular moment, though, the resemblance was uncanny. Ford felt like he was standing next to Emily.


Bailey napped in the guest room. Ford paid bills and went through his inventory. Grace's piece leaned against the wall next to the fireplace. He hadn't contacted her. He knew better. He also knew the collage needed a title. A title would make it Bailey's. Ford flipped through his final copy of *The Waste Land.* In the process of creating the collage he had purchased several editions, tearing out pages to create a mesh that he applied to the canvas and subsequently painted over. A technique he'd borrowed from Jane Fellow. The subliminal, she called it. Messages beneath the wax. Or in his case, beneath the acrylic and print.

He hadn't seen Jane in quite some time. He hadn't seen anyone really, outside of Lenny and Grace. And Bailey now too. But Grace was gone. He knew this. And yet he now feared she might linger if he didn't title her former collage.

He continued to thumb through *The Waste Land,* revisiting old friends. Certain lines popped but none stuck. He played White Elephant on his phone. Midway through the opening track, the work's elusive title presented itself.

Bailey emerged from the hallway. Ford pulled out his earplugs.

"What are out doing?" Bailey asked.

"I forgot to write the title," Ford said. He took the work to the kitchen table, removing a marker from the cabinet drawer.

"Here," Ford said, handing his son the canvas. "This is for you."

"*Fear in a handful of dust*," Bailey said, reading the title aloud.

"You like it?" Ford asked.

Bailey looked at his father, then back at the title. He turned the canvas over, studying the collage. "It's dope," he said.

# CHAPTER 14

An evening rainstorm turned into a brief snow flurry as they pulled into Eden's parking lot. Inside, Grace's barstool was empty. The place was relatively dead. A handful of people lingered at the bar, half of them with their backs to the stage. Three other men sat together at a high top, watching the lone stripper dance. Bailey took the place in, letting out an audible sigh. He made his way to the bathroom.

Ford couldn't say for sure who had led whom. Bailey awoke restless after his nap. And vocal about his restlessness. "I'm eighteen," he kept repeating, pacing the house. "I'm free. I can do whatever I want. What the fuck do I do now?"

The cocktail waitress arrived with a tray pressed into the side of her hip, the way a mother would carry an infant. Ford asked about Noire, a habit at this point. The waitress responded with a worn smile and absent eyes. Ford ordered a drink.

Alone, he eyed Grace's empty seat, aware then that like Noire this too would become an unbreakable habit. A dancer approached. She wore a red tie and black fedora, its low brim concealing her eyes.

"What you drinking, sweetie?"

"The waitress took care of it."

"You like sharing?" she asked.

"No," Ford said.

She leaned forward, revealing what little cleavage she had. The red tie brushed against Ford's nose. "Want to have you a little private dance?"

"My son's in the bathroom."

"Maybe grab him a dance once Layla finishes her routine."

"It's his birthday."

"Even more reason," she said. "We got a room full of mirrors right through them curtains." She pointed beyond the stage. "You're cute. I might even give you a deal."

"Maybe later."

"What if I told you it's already been paid for?"

"That goddamn kid," Ford said, turning in his chair to seek out his son.

"I'm sorry?" the woman asked.

"Bailey," he answered.

"No," she said, adjusting the fedora to reveal her pale blue eyes. "Ruth."

A gap divided her front teeth.

"Who?" Ford asked.

"My name's not Bailey, it's Ruth."

"Bailey's my son," Ford said. "The one who paid you."

"That ain't who paid me."

The cocktail waitress delivered Ford's drink. Ruth sat down at the table.

"Listen," she said, leaning forward. "Don't go looking behind you, but there's a man at the bar wanting me to give you this dance."

Ford turned around, expecting to find Bailey. Instead, he found JR. Ruth tugged on Ford's wrist, insisting he stop looking that way. JR scanned the room, making an effort to ignore Ford's attention. When he finally cracked, his quick glance widened with surprise before he approached the table.

"Ford?" he said, as if offended.

Whatever JR's plan had been, it was falling apart. His tongue ran back and forth behind his bottom row. His forehead perspired.

"You all know each other?" Ruth asked.

Bailey emerged from the bathroom. He lingered in the background, unsure what to make of the crowd.

"I thought you were a colleague," JR said to Ford. He turned to Ruth. "Why don't you go, I mistook him for someone else."

"He was coming for the dance," Ruth insisted. "Weren't you?"

JR placed money in her hand. "For your time and my confusion," he said, folding her fingers over the cash.

Ruth walked off, counting the bills.

Bailey sat down at the table. His appearance startled JR.

"My son," Ford explained.

JR nodded hello. "I know your father," he said.

Bailey nodded back, unimpressed. JR studied Bailey's face.

"It was good seeing you, JR," Ford said.

Rather than accept the farewell, JR joined the table, seating himself between father and son. "You live here?" he asked Bailey.

"No," Ford answered for his son. "He's visiting."

"I vaguely remember now," JR said. "Your father and I know each other."

"I vaguely remember now," Bailey mocked.

JR laughed, scanning the club. "Kind of a shithole here, huh? I mean you never really notice how dumpy a place is until you're with someone you know. Then suddenly you're seeing it through their eyes. Trying to see how they see it and how they might see you in it."

"If you don't like it, maybe you ought to call it a night," Ford said.

JR grinned. "My wife's a big fan of your father's work," he told Bailey. "He's a talented man, your father. But you probably know all this." He looked at Ford. "I don't need to tell him everything, do I?"

"No," Ford said. "You don't."

JR threw his head back and laughed, pressing his hand into his chest to emphasize his delight.

Ruth was introduced onstage. The opening bell toll for AC/DC's "Hell's Bells" rang out. Ruth stood with her back to the audience, easing her way to the floor.

"God this place is grimy," JR said, shaking his head. He rested his elbows on the table. "Do you know how much filth is on a dollar bill?" he asked. "Yet that's all anybody's after—

filth. You ever notice that? We're only interested in filth. That's what we should call it. Wouldn't that be something? To ask someone how much filth they have."

The cocktail waitress approached to see if she could grab JR a drink. To Ford's relief he declined.

"They try to get you drunk here so they can take all your filth," he told them once the cocktail waitress left. "I only ever have the club soda. But then they look at you like you're some kind of faggot. But see that's what they want you to do. They want you to drink. To make bad decisions. That's how they get all your filth."

JR's eyes remained on Ruth throughout his rant. She removed her fedora. A thick mane of dark red hair cascaded down her shoulders and back.

"Meanwhile, half the guys in here are faggots," JR continued. He turned to Bailey. "Did you know that?"

Bailey stared at JR blankly.

"What's wrong with you?" JR asked.

"We killed a possum the other day," Bailey answered.

JR turned to Ford for an explanation. Ford sipped his drink. JR looked back at Bailey. "What does that mean?"

Bailey didn't respond. JR repeated the question.

"It means we killed a possum," Ford answered.

"What's that got to do with anything?" JR asked.

"What's anything got to do with anything?" Bailey shot back, staring at the stage. "Besides, you just fucking talk, dude. Talk, talk, talk."

"You're very rude," JR said.

"Grumble, grumble, grumble," Bailey chanted.

"Is this what fatherhood is?" JR asked Ford.

"He doesn't fucking know," Bailey said, facing JR.

JR looked at Ford.

"Yeah, I guess so," Ford answered JR.

"How old are you?" JR asked Bailey.

"Old enough to fuck your wife," Bailey said.

JR's lip twitched. "If it wasn't for your father, I'd have already broken your face."

Bailey stood, nearly knocking over his chair. "I'll give you the first swing, hands behind my back."

"Sit down," Ford said.

"You'd let him," Bailey accused Ford.

JR remained seated, unimpressed. Bailey walked off to the bar.

"You need to go," Ford told JR.

"Your son isn't right."

"You need to go," Ford repeated.

"I'm being serious," he said. "There's something wrong with him."

"If you don't get the fuck out of here—"

"Have they met?" JR asked. "He and my wife?"

The question wasn't meant to antagonize. It was simply a question. Ford's silence provided the answer.

"Was he this spastic with her?"

"No," Ford said.

JR turned in his seat to examine Bailey from afar. "They met last night, I take it."

"What are you still doing here, JR?"

JR turned back around. "You and I are a lot alike," he said. "Self-sabotaging. I suppose that's why my wife liked you." He paused, looking over Ford. "She's come back to me, you know? It was all very sudden. Last night. I figured—well, I don't know what I figured. I guess I always figured she would. But it's been nagging me. The specifics, you know?"

JR's words gutted Ford. He felt hollow. The room suddenly distant. The music muffled. His face numb.

Bailey returned with a whiskey in one hand and a club soda in the other. He slid the latter to JR, who barked with laughter.

"He's very funny," JR said, pointing at Bailey with a stiff index finger. "I get it now."

Bailey sipped his whiskey without a word.

JR stood. "I need to go. It was a pleasure meeting you, Bailey. If you're ever in Houston and need a place to stay, my wife and I would love to have you."

JR stuck out his hand.

"You're fucking weird, dude," Bailey said, before accepting his farewell.

JR pointed at the stage. "That woman has a lot of my money for very little work. If either of you are interested, remind her of this when she finishes up."

"You mean filth," Bailey said.

"Excuse me?" JR asked.

"Money," Bailey reminded him.

"Of course," JR said with a crooked grin. "This was a very special place for me." He rapped his knuckles three times against the table. "I won't miss it."

Onstage, Ruth transitioned from grinding the floor to AC/DC's "Hell's Bells," to sailing around the pole to Metallica's "Enter Sandman."

Ford remained in a trance. He knew he'd lost Grace. He knew this before JR's declaration. Yet the confirmation drained him.

The cocktail waitress approached, insisting Bailey order all drinks through her.

"I got thirsty," he told her.

"You're in my section."

"You just want my money," he said.

"Yeah," she confirmed.

Bailey didn't initially respond. "We saw a dead possum the other day," he told her.

The cocktail waitress considered Bailey's words. "It could have been playing possum," she said.

Bailey eyed her for a moment. "You're quick, aren't you?"

"It could have been," she insisted.

Bailey shook his head. "Its ears were oozing blood."

"That's gross," she said.

"We saved it," Bailey assured her.

Her eyes softened.

205

Bailey pointed at Ford. "That guy ran it over."

She grimaced. Bailey laughed.

"You want another?" she asked.

Bailey nodded.

"How about you?"

Ford didn't answer.

"You want another?" she repeated.

Ford declined.

"You need to slow down," he told his son, once they were alone. Bailey scanned the room, ignoring him. Ford pulled out his cell phone to text Grace.

"Who was that guy?" Bailey asked.

Ford stared at his screen. Bailey repeated the question.

"Nobody," Ford said, canceling the message.

"How do you know him then?"

"His wife bought a collage."

"She a babe?"

"I hardly know her."

"So?"

"It's your birthday," Ford reminded him. "Let's talk about you."

Bailey raised his empty glass. Ford did the same.

"Eye contact," Bailey reminded him. "You can't make a toast without eye contact."

Ford was suddenly grateful to have his son there with him. "Neither of us has any beverage left to toast."

Bailey shrugged, tapping his father's empty glass. He then stood, lurching toward the blonde dancer at the side of the stage. The two watched Ruth dance a moment longer before Bailey whispered into the blonde's ear. She nodded and the two made their way into the private room behind the curtain.

The cocktail waitress returned with Bailey's drink.

"Not mine," Ford said.

She pointed at Bailey's empty seat. "It's for the one that kept talking about the possum."

Ford handed her a twenty and slid the drink back her way. "Do me a favor and take this with you and don't serve him again."

She left with Bailey's glass and Ford's money. Without thinking, Ford dialed Grace. It rang five times before going to voicemail. He called again. Straight to voicemail.

Ruth rejoined him at the table, her skin moist from her performance. Ford slid his phone inside his pocket.

"How do you know that man?" she asked, pointing to where JR previously sat.

"I don't."

"Okay, but how do you?"

"I sold a collage to his wife."

She twisted a strand of her red hair around her index finger. "What do you know about the wife?"

"Not much," he said.

She simpered. "You fucking her?"

Ford looked past Ruth toward the private lounge. Ruth laughed, reclaiming his attention. "Y'all are weirder than hell."

"I'm not fucking her," he said.

She continued to wind her red hair around her finger.

"You know him?" Ford asked, eyeing JR's former chair.

She closed her eyes, nodding her head pensively. "Best paying customer I ever had. Weirder than all hell, but weirdness comes with the territory." She freed her finger and crossed her hands. "Y'all look at us like we ain't even human."

"You look at us about the same."

"Chicken and the egg."

"What do you know?" he asked.

"I know the wife," she said. "The one you're not fucking."

Ford didn't say anything.

"And I know she paid me fifty bucks for what you're trying to get here for free."

Ford pulled out his wallet. He had two tens and a five.

"That don't even cover the dance."

"I'm not asking you to dance."

"You don't think I'm pretty?"

"You're beautiful."

"You fucking the wife?" she asked.

"That'll cost *you* fifty bucks."

She smiled and took his money. "He come in here a while back," she began. "The husband. And I give him a dance, and he starts talking the whole way through about what all I do and eventually he gets to asking if I do private shows for couples, and I tell him I do everything and he nods and I keep dancing and a few minutes later he says, what about groups? And I ask him what he means by groups and he says he's got a bachelor party for a friend coming up and he wants to know if I'd dance for the whole group of them. I tell him not in the room we was in. And he says, why not? And I say, 'cause it ain't big enough—which it ain't. I say, we ain't got the room for fifteen men. And he shakes his head and says it ain't no fifteen men. Says it'd just be him and his buddy. And I say, I suppose I could but why not just get his buddy a private dance? I tell him I'd make it worth his buddy's wild. Well, the thing is, he says, I want to play a joke on my buddy. He says, he ain't really my buddy. He says it's his future brother-in-law. Says he thinks the man is marrying his sister for the money. Says he's convinced the man's a homo and he wants to prove it. Tells me if I'm willing, he'll pay me as much as I need and all I got to do is have the two of them come in with me so I can dance for them both before leaning into his future brother-in-law's ear and whispering that he ought to touch the husband's crotch.

"Now it was strange and maybe he seen it in my eyes because he starts backpedaling. But this here ain't fucking church. I mean I seen things. And considering the money, I tell him sure. And so the next week the husband comes in with his future brother-in-law and I whisper in the man's ear like I was told and the man laughs and shakes his head and that's the end of it. I finish dancing for them both and the husband and the man leave.

"But then a few days later he comes back with a different man. He finds me on his own and hands me the money up-front and says, same as last time. Says, come grab us at the bar in fifteen. He's real fast the way he talks. Kind of nervous. Says he'll give me an extra hundred if I insist this time. He don't wait to hear my answer. Hands me the hundred right there and repeats the fact that I should meet him and the man at the bar in fifteen.

"So I do. I bring 'em both in the back and I whisper in the man's ear to go on and grab a hold of his buddy's crotch. At first the man sort of just laughs it off. Meanwhile, the husband pretends he don't know what's going on. Says, what are you two whispering over there? And I tell him, don't you worry, and he sort of looks at me. Then he holds up a fifty and places it on me. So I insist. I tell the other man, go on and touch it. I tell him, you touch it and I'll touch you. By then the man is real nervous. But he keeps looking at my breasts and every so often over at the husband, and I mean they're sitting two feet apart, but he says to me, I ain't going nothing inside the pants. And I just nod because the husband ain't said how he wanted to be touched, so I just assume I've done all I was brought there for. And so the man reaches over and grabs hold of the husband's crotch and the husband shoots up real fast and starts barking at this guy, calling him a faggot and threatening to kick his ass and telling him to get the fuck out. Well, the guy looks at me and I just shrug and he races on out and the husband sort of just sits there like he's shocked. And then he tells me, can you believe that faggot? Course, I don't know what to make of none of it until the husband slides another fifty my way and tells me to go on and grind up on him. And so I do, and he leaves soon enough with his pants all wet.

"And so that's how we've been doing things now for close to three, four weeks. Every couple days he comes in with somebody or picks one out for me to grab. Most of the guys, they ain't willing. But a few always are."

Ruth looked over the room, shaking her head.

"But see then there's this one guy last week—I didn't have to ask him twice. He reaches right over for the husband's crotch and when the husband stands and calls him a faggot, the guy don't run out all humiliated-like. Instead, he stands there and accuses the husband of being the faggot. Says, don't go pretending my hand caught you by surprise. Course, the husband is near belligerent. Threatening to kill the man and kick his ass, until finally our bouncer Eddie comes in and tries to take the husband out, but I stand up for him, you know, because—and I ain't proud of it, per se—but three of his visits cover my month's rent. So I tell Eddie to kick out the other man, and once he's gone the husband sinks down into the booth and just stares off for a minute. Then he starts shaking a little, telling me it ain't right. That he feels sick. And I try and console him and all, but he tells me no, so I give him his space and he sort of works himself through it, pinching the bridge of his nose, breathing all heavy and that kind of stuff. And then just as soon as it came, it left, and he sort of spins his finger in the air at me like, well, come on and take care of this. So I sit on top of him and I grind up in his lap and we finish things off like we usually do."

She rested her chin in the palm of her hand. "Tires me out, just thinking about it."

"What about Grace?" Ford asked.

Ruth stared. "Who?"

"Grace," he repeated. "The wife."

She leaned back in her chair. "I ain't accustomed to talking so much," she said.

"I don't have any more cash."

"That's not what I meant," she said. "I'm just stating a fact."

She paused to gather her thoughts. "She's pretty, the wife. You get some like that from time to time. They come in here with their husbands—sometimes for him, sometimes for her, most times for both. I've lost count of how many couples try and take me home."

For a moment, Ford thought she was actually calculating past requests.

"Grace," Ruth said, taking in the name. "She never come in here with the husband. First few times she don't say nothing. Asks how much it'll cost for a dance, pays it, and then just sits there. Was hard to gauge her the way she stared. I could tell she was trying to figure me out some and that sort of made me nervous-like, but then after the third or fourth visit it's like you get used to the way someone acts until it don't scare you no more, and then finally it's like you almost like it and once that happens you want to try and figure it out. Like why is it that you are the way you are kind of thing."

"And so that's how it happens. I tell her, sweetie, you've become one of my regulars now and it's sort of strange, seeing as I don't know nothing about you. And that's when she asks what's going on with the men who are always in here before me. At this point, it's kind of exciting, you know? Like her talking is some kind of victory on my end. So I kind of celebrate by having fun with it. Dancing a bit on her, being flirty, 'cause now that she is talking it feels more natural. So I say, sweetie, what happens in here I don't never tell nobody. Still being flirty-like, you know? Just to keep it going. But that's when she drops the act. Says, that man is my husband. And see I ain't expecting nothing like that. I mean I literally cover myself up. I really did. 'Cause I ain't had no clue this whole time who this woman was.

"Course, then she holds up a fifty and just says talk. And now believe it or not but I'm nervous. Not because I know all this stuff about her husband that she don't, but 'cause he wet his pants with me a dozen times by then and for whatever reason that's all I kept thinking about. Like that'd be the thing to upset her the most. Course, it ain't like that's something I tell her about. But I tell her everything else. Everything I just told you. And she starts crying some. And so like an idiot I start yapping. Telling her things to try and make it so her husband don't seem so weird. Which I suppose he ain't. I mean I've had people in here wanting me to use lollypops, spoons—anything they could put in their mouths after. Folks telling me stuff about themselves like this here's confession.

"But that ain't what she's crying about. Once she calms down some and gets hold of her breath, she tells me it's sad. She don't say much of anything else, but she didn't really have to, you know? It's like you just never know. Even when you think you do you still don't."

For a moment neither spoke.

"What'd you say your name was?" she asked.

"Ford."

"That your first name?"

He nodded.

"Sort of unusual," she said. "I like it, though. Very noble. The husband won't tell me his name. Didn't mind it at first, but now it's almost like I resent him for it. Like we have us something here and I don't even really know who he is."

"Jeffrey Burnett," Ford said. "People call him JR."

She considered the information. "Well, that's too bad."

"You don't like the name?"

"Name's fine," she said. "Was kind of hoping he'd've been the one to tell it."

"Well, they're gone now," Ford said.

"Next time he comes in, I mean."

"No, I'm saying they're gone," he said. "They're going back to Houston."

Ford didn't know this until he spoke it. Then it became apparent. It became a fact. The Burnetts were going back to Houston.

"No," Ruth said.

"Yes," Ford insisted, more to himself than to her.

"He'd've told me something like that," she said.

214

"Why?" Ford asked, hoping her answer might prove him wrong.

"Because," she said, looking around the place. "I was good to him."

"You gave him up for fifty bucks."

"That don't mean I wasn't good to him," she said. "I treated him right."

Ford didn't know what to say. The Burnetts were going back to Houston.

"Y'all treat us like we ain't even human," she said.

A shout came from the back room. Ford nearly knocked over the table as he rushed toward it. The pale blonde shot out from behind the curtain. Vomit slid off her chest.

Inside the private lounge, Bailey sat slouched on a velvet couch with an erection tenting his pants and vomit on his shirt. He grunted as Ford leaned over to pick him up.

"He with you?" the bouncer asked Ford.

"No," Ford said, sliding Bailey's arm over his shoulder. "I just thought it'd be fun to do your fucking job."

The bouncer didn't know how to respond. "Yeah, well get him the fuck out of here," he finally said.


Ford cleaned his son off at a nearby gas station. Bailey's dry tongue kept running over his dry lips. Ford had him drink two bottles of water. They sat in his car underneath the station's florescent lights. Ford eventually went back inside to grab Bailey a coffee. The attendant followed Ford outside, watching him and Bailey from the doorway. He soon tapped on Ford's window, telling him they needed to go.

The car's movement upset Bailey. They ended up in the parking lot at a nearby Waffle House. Bailey's eyes gradually opened. A slow smile spread across his face. He wanted a Grand Slam.

Ford shook his head. "This isn't Denny's."

"Grand Slam," Bailey repeated in a slow whisper. "It's my birthday."

Ford had his son recite the alphabet. Bailey took his time. Ford then asked him to touch his nose. Bailey's finger found its way to the apparatus. Ford told him if he threw up pancakes, he was on his own. It took his son a moment, but he located the door handle and slid out.

Ford called Grace. It went to voicemail. Bailey continued toward the diner. Ford lingered in the parking lot, the asphalt wet from the earlier snow flurry. He tried Grace's number again. Bailey turned around, nearly slipping on a small patch of ice.

"Stop calling here," Grace whispered into the receiver.

Ford waved Bailey inside.

"I met your husband tonight," he told her.

"You've already met," she told him back.

"Yeah, well, I met Ruth tonight too," he said.

"I imagine Bailey had a good time."

Ford looked toward the diner. Inside, the waitress approached Bailey, who smiled, miming a baseball player at bat.

"Why'd you come to dinner?" Ford asked Grace, still staring at his son through the window.

"I wanted to meet him."

"Even though you were leaving."

"Was I?"

"You are."

"Well, you know everything, don't you?"

"He tried buying me a lap dance," Ford told her. "Your husband."

"I don't care," she said.

"What do you think'll happen back in Houston?"

"What do you think will happen right now?" she said. "There's nothing you can tell me that I don't already know."

A couple entered the Waffle House. Bailey stretched his neck to see if it was Ford. His boy then pressed his face against the diner's window. Ford waved, holding up his finger to let his son know he was on his way. He then turned his back on Bailey.

"Why'd you want to meet my son?" he asked. "If you were leaving this whole time?"

"I can't do this," she said. "I'm hanging up."

"Tell me," he said. "You owe me that much."

"He's your son," she said.

"Yeah, I know."

"Your child."

"And I'm his father."

217

Ford waited for her to respond. She was silent for some time. "But you aren't a good one," she said.

Ford ended the call.


The food arrived shortly after Ford joined Bailey at the table. Bailey looked over the stack of pancakes, overwhelmed by its size. The waitress asked if she could grab Ford anything. He ordered a cup of coffee and saw about getting a spare plate.

The two worked on the pancakes in silence. Ford's phone rang. Bailey eyed the screen. Ford put it on vibrate. Bailey didn't ask. They continued to fill their mouths with the late-night meal.


In the car, Bailey rubbed his hands together. Ford cranked the heat.

"You all right?" he asked.

"I'm freezing," Bailey said.

"It's warming up."

Bailey dug through his pockets and pulled out his phone. He connected it to the car's input. Ambient noise filled the space, accompanied by bongos and the fading notes of a sax. Then it all dropped, replaced by layered vocals singing to a sharp bass line.

"Who is this?" Ford asked.

"Are you kidding me?"

"No."

"Arcade Fire," Bailey said.

"This is *not* Arcade Fire."

Bailey held up his phone to show Ford the cover: a marble statue of a naked man, eyes shielded, with a woman connected to him. It didn't say the band's name anywhere.

"David Bowie's on this track," Bailey said.

Ford adjusted the volume. "It doesn't sound like them."

"How have you not heard this album?"

"Didn't *The Suburbs* just come out?"

"Like forever ago," Bailey said. "You introduced me to these guys."

"I did not."

"You made me go to their concert."

"That was for your birthday."

"I was like ten," Bailey said.

Ford didn't have the energy or certainty to argue it. "This doesn't even sound like them," he repeated.

"They're evolving," Bailey said.

"I don't hear Bowie."

"He comes later," Bailey promised, lowering the volume. "Listen, I need to talk to you."

Bailey amazed Ford. If it wasn't for the pink stains marking his son's jacket, Ford never would have guessed Bailey had had a single drink that night, much less regurgitated those same drinks onto the chest of a stripper. He nodded at his son, inviting him to go on.

"It's about my brand," Bailey said.

"Your *brand?*"

"I'm getting sponsored," he said. "By Flash Boards. Tim's working out the contract now."

For a moment, Ford didn't know who Tim was. He'd been Shark Man for so long. "What's he charging you?"

"Why would he charge me?" Bailey asked.

"I'm kidding."

"Tim says it's not like a fortune-fortune. But fuck, it's like over a hundred grand. Maybe not after taxes, but that's still a shit ton of money. And like Buddha says, this is just the start. I'm doing that video with Buddha next month. He's got like over half a million followers. I'm at like forty-five thousand. But once this video comes out it's gonna like blow me up."

Ford wasn't sure how to respond. He was happy for his son. Grateful that Bailey was the one to deliver the news. Amazed that Emily hadn't taken this moment away from him.

"Just don't let it go to your head," Ford said.

Bailey huffed. "I just told you I'm getting sponsored."

"I know," Ford said.

Bailey turned up the music.

"Hey," Ford said, lowering it.

Bailey stared out the window. "I'm changing my name," he said.

Ford laughed. The topic was an old favorite. Bailey had been threatening to change his name since he was little. Back then he lamented over its androgyny. For a brief period he insisted on going by his middle name, Hunter. Until he discovered its androgyny as well.

"What's it gonna to be this time?" Ford asked. "Carl? Ryan? Andrew? Steve? Oh, I know—Devon, right? Devon Walk—"

"Warwick," Bailey interrupted.

It didn't initially register. "Warwick Carson?"

"Bailey Warwick."

Ford's phone vibrated inside his pocket.

"You gonna say something?" Bailey asked.

Ford's chest tingled. The sensation moved to the back of his throat and made its way to the front of his forehead. The music seemed stuck on a single phrase, an increasing panic of the words: *just a reflection*. But then it stopped.

Ford took out his phone. He had a notification. He punched in his passcode, but he entered it wrong.

"Who are you texting?"

Ford punched in his passcode again. Grace's text read: *We both made mistakes. I shouldn't have said what I said. I don't want to end things*

"I'm talking to you," Bailey said.

Ford placed his phone between his legs. It vibrated again.

Grace wrote: *you two are the same. That's always what makes it hard.*

Her messages were out of order. He scrolled up to the first text, but it didn't connect.

Bailey pulled the wheel. Ford dropped his phone.

"What are you doing?" Ford shouted.

"Getting your fucking attention."

Ford combed the floor with his foot. The phone vibrated underneath his shoe.

"Are you gonna say something?" Bailey asked.

His son's words were a plea. Ford knew whatever he said next, he could never unsay. He wanted it to be right. To be measured. He wanted his son to know he understood. That there wasn't anything else that Bailey needed to say. He was a bad father; Timothy was the better man.

His phone vibrated a fourth time.

But Ford couldn't speak. He was neither living nor dead. Just hurt. What he told his son was a result of his hurt. Ford was like a child in this way. He only knew how to stop hurt by making others hurt. Later on, he'd try and convince himself otherwise. And for a period he'd believe it. He'd believe that what he told Bailey was meant to help assuage his son's own inevitable guilt. Because certainly Bailey would feel guilty about changing his name. He'd maybe even regret it.

"She's pregnant," Ford said.

The statement originated as a lie. To let Bailey know that he too was replaceable. But once spoken, the truth of the matter could not be ignored.

"She's pregnant," Ford said, repeating the revelation.

"What the hell are you talking about?"

"Grace," he shouted. "She's pregnant."

"I'm changing my name," Bailey screamed.

Ford reached down for his phone. Bailey's words filled the car. Ford's thumb dialed in his passcode. The remainder of the texts appeared. Four more, out of order.

The first one read: *Goodbye Ford.* He scrolled down to the next one: *that way. But there's no easy way to end this. Sometimes we have to pretend. That's something I never wanted*

Bailey's words filled the car, but Ford didn't hear them. He scrolled to the next message, trying to figure out the proper arrangement*: to believe. None of this is ideal. But it's manageable. I'm turning off my phone after this. I think it will be for the best.*

The final text read: *Bailey should be your priority. He's very much like you. More vocal, perhaps. But*

The silence was what pulled Ford away from his screen. The car was soundless. But then the noise came rushing back. The music blared. Bailey's voice blasted. But none of what his son said made any sense. He was speaking broken English.

Until it hit Ford: Bailey was crying. Violently. His forehead rested on the dash. His hands pressed over his ears as if his son couldn't stand the sound of his own tears.

Ford reached out to touch his boy. To try and make it stop. To apologize.

He would not remember the rest. Except for his knee. His knee was steering the wheel. And his phone. He had his phone in his left hand while his right hand reached out for Bailey. There was no impact. No sound. No pain from shattered bones. But it all happened. He wouldn't remember any of it, but that's how it goes.

# EPILOGUE

His knee required a full year of rehab. Within that period, he and Lenny lost their lease. The building's owner had expanded his son's downstairs wine bar, converting it into a fine dining establishment. They made it a point to emphasize the fact that they designated a portion of the back wall for local artists to sell their work. Meanwhile, the son took fifty percent of all sales. Two of the upstairs spaces were still used as galleries. The rest had been converted into a coworking space.

Ford and Lenny found separate, smaller studios within the district. Lenny worked in a section of a basement inside a building that used to be an icehouse. Ford's new space was above a brewery.

Despite the location, Ford gave up drinking. For a period, Lenny joined him in sobriety. They met up for coffee, treating it like an informal AA meeting. Inevitably, their conversations reverted to speculation: How much longer did either think they had before their new studio space would be converted into a boutique shop or a hair salon? Overtime they saw less of each other, until finally neither made the effort.

The Warwicks returned to Florida shortly after the accident. Emily wanted to be closer to family. Her mother still lived in Dania. It helped.

Ford flew in every couple of weeks. He mentioned the idea of moving back during one of these visits. Emily and

Timothy both encouraged the idea. The three spoke regularly over the phone. They never brought up the accident. Because it was an accident.

This bothered Ford at first. The fact that the seventeen-year-old driver and his girlfriend claimed black ice. Ford didn't want to believe it. Because it gave him an out. He tried remembering the impact, but he couldn't. The official report confirmed black ice. And so that was that. It was black ice.

His phone survived the collision. Not even a scratch on its screen. More than the black ice, it bothered Ford that he unscrambled her message.

It read:

> *We both made mistakes. I shouldn't have said what I said. I don't want to end things that way. But there's no easy way to end this. Sometimes we have to pretend. That's something I never wanted to believe. None of this is ideal. But it's manageable. I'm turning off my phone after this. I think it will be for the best. Bailey should be your priority. He's very much like you. More vocal, perhaps. But you two are the same. That's always what makes it hard. Goodbye Ford.*

For months after the crash, Bailey's collage remained leaning against the wall. Ford didn't know what to do with it. He certainly didn't want anybody else to have it. He thought about destroying it. But then what if Bailey asked for it one of these days?

Eventually, Ford hung it above the mantle, replacing Jane Fellow's encaustic wave. He spent many sleepless nights studying the piece. It was during one of these hypnotic sessions that Ford realized how to find her. He typed *Evelyn Grace* in the Facebook search key. Her profile setting offered limited access. But there she was staring right at him, with JR on her left, his hand placed at the bottom of her protruding belly.

If Ford didn't know any better he would have assumed they were a young, happy couple entering the next great phase of their life. Because that's what pictures like that conveyed. And that's what people loved to see. Happiness. In fact, one hundred and thirty-three people liked to see this particular couple's happiness. And maybe they were happy. They looked happy.

For two weeks, Ford returned to her page nightly. And for two weeks, he studied this young, happy couple entering the next great phase of their life. Did JR know? Would it even matter if he did? Ford scrutinized Grace's smile. Was it real? Was she real? Were they real? No, he decided. They were just strangers—a pair of young, happy strangers entering the next great phase of their life.

Ford deleted his Facebook account.


Stem cell research. Ford found a clinic in Mexico. Emily and Timothy found one in Germany. They discussed the possibility of flying out to either location that December.

"Let's talk more the next time you're here," Emily told Ford over the phone.

226

"That's next week, correct?" Timothy asked over the speaker.

"The following," Ford corrected him.


His travels south grew more frequent. On each visit, he'd roll Bailey onto the sand and lift him out of his chair. His son moaned sometimes. But usually he just stared. On occasion, Ford convinced himself that he saw Bailey smiling. And in those moments, Ford told himself that his son was somewhere else—grateful that Bailey had seen as much of the world as he had.

On his most recent visit, the sun was just beginning to rise as he and Bailey approached the sand. Bailey looked toward the horizon. His lifeless limbs hung at his sides. A few morning riders were already on the water. Ford carried Bailey toward the shoreline.

"You're heavy, you know that?" Ford told him. "When did you get so heavy?" he teased.

Bailey moaned.

Ford stood before the ocean with his son in his arms, studying the break. He lowered them onto the wet sand, arranging Bailey between his knees. The dying waves stretched out toward them, gliding over their ankles and wetting the backs of their pants.

"That'll be you again soon enough," Ford said, pointing toward the surfers. He told this to his son on every visit. "But don't go telling everybody, okay? Let's let it be our little secret. Our big surprise."

The sky began to glow a bright orange.

Bailey again moaned.

"What's the matter?"

Bailey sat still.

"I was kidding, you know?" Ford said. "Tell anyone you want. Hell, everybody already knows."

The sky continued to brighten.

"Do you remember when you were little?" Ford asked. "You had that lisp and you'd run around the beach calling out about the waves. You'd scream, *They're cwaashing, daddy! They're cwaashing!*" Ford laughed. "Do you remember?"

Bailey stared out onto the water.

"You're my baby, you know that?" Ford said. "My one and only."

A seagull glided above them, wings spread, spiraling in the wind. The pair sat silent, a father and son watching the riders paddle beyond the break to catch their first wave of the day—that dream ride that always seems a stroke away. It's the reason you keep going, convinced you'll never stop, until your arms give out just as the water begins to rise, leaving you to witness the results of those long ago winds, forgotten sounds, an unknowable past indifferent to your anticipation, your joy, your relief. Tired hands work in tandem with tired knees. Your feet set. The wave rushes beneath you. And then just like that, it's gone.

# ACKNOWLEDGEMENTS

Thank you Tyson Morgan for helping me to figure out the best way to tell this story. I resisted some of your advice early on and it cost me a few years and several drafts.

Thank you Kristen Marckmann and the entire Unsolicited team.

Thank you to all my Texas friends, colleagues and professors at the University of Houston who contributed to my development as a writer and person: Alex Parsons, Robert Boswell, Antonya Nelson, Chitra Banerjee Divakaruni, Mat Johnson, Zachary Martin, Erin Mushalla, Justin Chrestman, Josette Arvizu, Claire Anderson, Sara Rolater, Elizabeth Winston, Nancy Pearson, Peter Kimani, Dickson Lam, Jameelah Lang, Whit Bones, Austin Tremblay, Michelle Mariano, Nathan Graham, JP Gritton, Aja Gabel, Celeste Prince, Corey Noll, Peter Graham, Heather Sartin, Katie Condon, Danny "Set Play" Wallace, Joseph "Boot Brother" Scapellato, Conor and Rachel Bracken, Henk Rossouw, Tavia Lee-Goldstein, Julia Brown, Steve Sanders, Dee Bartham, Will Donnelly, Ian Stansel, Selena Anderson, Brad Parrigin, Whitney Mower, Will Wilkinson, Karyna McGlynn, Talia Mailman, Antonio Elefano, Justin Ploof, the entire WITS team and Inprint.

Thank you to my writer pals outside of Houston: Zach Powers, Karen O'Donnell Krajcer, PJ Devlin, Bobby Sauro and BANKER!

Thank you to David Wood, Matthew Langley, Mrs. Carter, and Jessica Livingston.

Many thanks to the Wolfe Pack, Gina Smith, Dan Hesse, the Xpress team, Don & Cece, Nick & Dana, Linda & Mike.

Thank you Chase McGee for your time, feedback and encouragement. (And thank you Ramona and Rory for keeping Chase in check.)

Thank you Riva Babies: Nir Ben Jacob, Natalie Spoden Ben Jacob, Elia Ben Jacob, Robert Cernuda, Vanessa Cunto, Lara Calloway, Kyle Bretz and Megan Stewart.

Thank you to my family: Momma Joanie and Dad—you two make it all possible; Dee, Lindsay, Madden, Linden Jane and the rest of the Calders and Knights; Celine Rivest and the late Palmer Drexel Fischbeck; Meg and John Calder.

Thank you Patapouf—every writer needs a good dog to talk to and walk with in between sessions, and you have gone above and beyond.

Thank you Eula for making life beautiful.

And above all, thank you Tatiana for being everything and making it all worthwhile. I love you.

# ABOUT THE AUTHOR

Thomas Calder's writing has appeared in *Gulf Coast, Miracle Monocle, The Collective Quarterly*, and elsewhere. He earned his MFA in creative writing at the University of Houston. He now lives in Asheville, N.C. with his wife, daughter and dog.

# ABOUT THE PRESS

Unsolicited Press was founded in 2012 and is based in Portland, Oregon. The small press publishes fiction, poetry, and creative nonfiction written by award-winning and emerging authors. Some of its authors include John W. Bateman, Anne Leigh Parrish, Adrian Ernesto Cepeda, and Raki Kopernik.

Learn more at www.unsolicitedpress.com